Books by Sid Fleischman

MR. MYSTERIOUS & COMPANY
BY THE GREAT HORN SPOON!
THE GHOST IN THE NOONDAY SUN
CHANCY AND THE GRAND RASCAL

Chancy and the Grand Rascal

CHANCY
and the
GRAND RASCAL

by Sid Fleischman

Illustrated by Eric von Schmidt

Joy Street Books
Little, Brown and Company
Boston • Toronto • London

COPYRIGHT © 1966 BY ALBERT S. FLEISCHMAN, INC.

ALL RIGHTS RESERVED. NO PART OF THIS BOOK MAY BE REPRODUCED IN ANY
FORM OR BY ANY ELECTRONIC OR MECHANICAL MEANS INCLUDING INFORMA-
TION STORAGE AND RETRIEVAL SYSTEMS WITHOUT PERMISSION IN WRITING
FROM THE PUBLISHER, EXCEPT BY A REVIEWER WHO MAY QUOTE BRIEF
PASSAGES IN A REVIEW.

LIBRARY OF CONGRESS CATALOG CARD NO. 66-14903

THE CHARACTERS AND EVENTS PORTRAYED IN THIS BOOK ARE FICTITIOUS.
ANY SIMILARITIES TO REAL PERSONS, LIVING OR DEAD, ARE COINCIDENTAL
AND NOT INTENDED BY THE AUTHOR.

ISBN: 0-316-28575-7 (hc)
ISBN: 0-316-26012-6 (pb)
10 9 8   (hc)
10 9 8 7 6 5 4 3 2 1 (pb)

Joy Street Books are published
by Little, Brown and Company (Inc.)

Published simultaneously in Canada
by Little, Brown & Company (Canada) Limited

PRINTED IN THE UNITED STATES OF AMERICA

For Pearl and Honey

Contents

Chancy and the Grand Rascal

1

The Buckeye Traveler

PUSHING his belongings in a squealing wheelbarrow Chancy set out for the Ohio River fifty miles away. He clicked his heels once or twice and began to whistle through his teeth. His travels had begun.

Dawn was aglow behind the buckeye trees and roosters were crowing for miles around. When he was out of sight of the Starbuck farmhouse he pulled off his shoes and added them to the load in the wheelbarrow. He didn't intend to wear out a new pair of shoes by walking in them.

The squeak of the old wheelbarrow raised blackbirds along the way. Chancy watched the passing sights with speckled green eyes — cat's eyes, folks called them. He had dark, lanky hair and a nose as thin as a hatchet. He was growing up tall and lean and limber-jointed, but strong as wire. Jody, his friend Jody Starbuck, was always saying:

"Chancy, if you was any skinnier you'd have to stand twice to throw a shadow."

That wasn't precisely true. He could see his shadow moving along the dusty wagon road, keeping him company. He was going to miss Jody, and the squire with his hearty laugh and Mrs. Starbuck. They had tried to make him one

of the family. But even among jolly, big-hearted folks like
the Starbucks he had felt apart and alone. He had a powerful yearning to find his own kin. Now that he was big
enough he was on his way at last. By dogs!

He stopped now and then to spit on his hands. The
wheelbarrow was infernally heavy. Mrs. Starbuck was
afraid he might starve along the way; it seemed to him she
had loaded him up with enough eats to last until he was
full grown. In addition to his bedroll he also had along his
Pa's four-pound axe and wedges. He prized that axe. It had
a fine black cherry handle and was all he owned that had
once belonged to his father.

The morning was heating up, but he stepped along
steady as a clock. All he had to do was head straight south
and he'd run smack into the Ohio River. Bound to.

4

Couldn't miss it, Squire Starbuck had told him. Then he'd climb aboard a big steamboat, pay his money and ride all the way to Paducah. That's where his sister was, as far as he knew. He aimed to hunt her up. His sister Indiana.

And after Indiana there would be Mirandy to find and little Jamie, too. Chancy was the oldest of the Dundee children and he reckoned that made him the head of the family.

It was four years ago that he had last seen his brother and sisters. After the death of their mother, the youngsters had been separated, scattered about the countryside like leaves on the wind. But all through those years Chancy told himself that when he grew big enough he'd set out and round them up, Indiana and Mirandy and little Jamie. He was the oldest, wasn't he? And kin belonged together, didn't they?

The sun was glowing overhead like a red-hot coal. Suddenly stones began dropping like meteors out of the clear Ohio sky. One, two, three, they raised blossoms of dust in the road ahead.

It gave Chancy a start. He squinted at the sky and then took a backward glance over his shoulder. There, with a handful of pebbles, stood a red-headed boy. A smile sprang toward Chancy's face, but he forced it back. He set down the hot handles of the wheelbarrow and turned.

"Jody Starbuck, if I ain't mistaken."

"You ain't."

"What in thunder are you doing way out here?"

"Throwing rocks."

Chancy tried to spit between his teeth, but his mouth

5

was too dry. "You turn around and go on home, Jody."

"Not likely."

"You ain't coming with me."

"Why not?"

Chancy took a deep breath. "Your Pa will be out looking for you."

"We got a right smart head start."

"I declare, Jody, do you think your Pa won't know where you lit out for?"

"I reckon I'd like to see the Ohio River with you, Chancy. And Paducah, and all those fine places you're a-goin'."

Chancy pushed back his straw hat and peered solemnly at the smaller boy standing in the road. He couldn't think of anyone he'd rather have along than his friend Jody. They had slept in the same feather bed for two years, and even though Chancy was older he always treated Jody Starbuck as an equal. But he couldn't let him run away.

"The Ohio River?" Chancy scoffed. "Why, that's nothing to see. I'm going to tell you the bottom truth, Jody — that river don't amount to a thing. It's just plain old ditch water strung out and trying to look important. You talk like you never seen water in your life. And it's full of alligators. I read that in the almanac, so you know I ain't making it up. Alligators are so thick this time of year they jump about like hoptoads. You take your life in your hands to come within ten miles of that old river."

"I'd like to see an alligator."

Chancy sighed and said, "Jody, you go on back, before the squire takes the hide off you."

Chancy lifted the handles of the wheelbarrow and

started forward. A few moments later stones were falling out of the sky again.

"You want me to push the barrow for you?" Jody called.

"I haven't even begun to get tired," Chancy said.

"Ma about changed her mind about letting you go."

"Did she?"

"She wanted Pa to fetch you back. But he said you had a bad case of the yonders, and there'd be no keeping you on the farm. He said you can't keep a squirrel on the ground."

Chancy headed into the shade of a buckeye tree and stopped. "You're following me like a cow's tail."

"Reckon."

"Jody, you're going home if I have to whip you first. But I guess you can eat with me, unless you ain't hungry."

"I'm hungry."

They rooted around in the wheelbarrow among the fresh biscuits and loaves of salt-rising bread, the jars of preserves, the jug of sweet cider, the hard-boiled eggs, the lump of beef out of the brine barrel, the pickles, the pies and the cold fried chicken. They started with a peach pie and ended with the cider.

Afterwards, they lay in the shade and Chancy looked over the fallen buckeyes scattered like brown marbles under the tree. Carrying a buckeye was good luck. He picked out a fat round one with a good white eye and began to polish it along the side of his nose.

"Hot, ain't it?" Jody said.

"I hardly noticed," Chancy answered. That wasn't strictly true. If it got any hotter the cornfield yonder would break into popcorn. By dogs it was hot, and summer just beginning.

"You remember your Pa?"

Chancy merely nodded. He never spoke much about his folks. The Civil War had come and gone and his father hadn't come back, and never would. But Chancy remembered him as clearly as if he were standing there in the road with his doctor bag. In earlier days, when the family was together, they lived up north in Erie County. His father had been killed in the Battle of Kenesaw Mountain, but Chancy could still call up the warm, robust sound of his voice. Sometimes, when he was just falling asleep, it came to Chancy as clear as a bell.

"What if you don't find your sister in Paducah?" Jody asked. "You reckon you'll toe it back here?"

"I reckon I'll just keep looking until I find her."

"How'd she ever get a name like Indiana?"

"That's where my Ma was from. I told you that."

"They named her after the state?"

"Jody, you're a bear for getting things turned around. Once Indiana was born they named the *state* after *her*."

When Chancy had the buckeye polished to a high, mahogany sheen he held it to the sun and studied the ghostly white eye. The war had changed everything. Some months after word came about his Pa, his mother had died of winter fever. Suddenly Chancy and his younger sisters and brother found themselves alone in the world.

A neighbor lady, Miss Russell, had tried to find homes for them. Indiana had been the first to be taken away, kicking like a wildcat and calling for Chancy at the top of her voice. He would never forget that day. A chair bottomer on his way to Paducah had offered to apprentice her and raise her. She'd be eleven now. Chancy remembered him as a turkey-necked man named Jones.

Chancy himself had been the next to go, leaving little Mirandy and Jamie behind. Where they might be living now he couldn't guess.

Chancy had gone to live in Sandusky with a harness maker. Through the years Chancy had been passed along from one family to another until he ended up with Jody's folks in the southern part of the state. All the while he had been marking time, waiting to grow up so he could strike out and find his blood kin.

Jody began cracking the joints in his toes. "How come you don't have any other folks?"

"I told you. There's Mirandy and little Jamie. He's the youngest."

"I mean grown-up kin."

Chancy slipped the buckeye into his hip pocket. It was time to get moving. "I used to have an uncle somewhere. He went out West a long time ago. My Uncle Will. Oh, he was a grand rascal, Mama used to say. But I reckon he got killed in the war too, or scalped by Indians maybe." Chancy got up. "Goodbye, Jody."

"I'm coming along."

"Are you going to make me whip you?"

"Reckon so."

Chancy slammed his hat to the ground. "Jody, you *know* I can lick you. You start for home."

Jody pulled in his neck and began rolling his fists. "You aim to whip me, or stand there talking all summer?"

Jody was calling his bluff and Chancy couldn't think what to do about it. He didn't want to hit Jody. He couldn't. But he couldn't let Jody come along, either.

"Jody, I declare! You don't have sense enough to pull in your head when you shut the window."

"I got sense enough to know there ain't no alligators in the Ohio River."

"Well," said Chancy, "I just don't have time to lick you, if you want to know the truth. I'm in a hurry."

"It won't take long."

"Jody, get back up that road! Hear me? I mean it! The squire will be out to fetch you before long, and you'll get a real hiding." Chancy's glance lit on his belongings in the wheelbarrow. "I'll tell you what I'll do. I'll give you my store-bought teeth."

Jody kept his fighting pose, but Chancy saw the effect of his miraculous offer. He dug through his odds and ends and unfolded a blue bandana. He held the false teeth up to the light of day and gave them a clack. Several teeth were broken off, which improved the sinister effect. Jody wanted this rare treasure. He always had. Chancy had found the teeth more than a year before, and when nobody claimed them the squire let him keep them. They were the envy of every boy in the county, and a guaranteed wonder for scaring girls.

"Go ahead and take them," Chancy said. "They're yours."

Jody lowered his fists. Chancy gave the teeth another clack and Jody took them in his hands. "Sure look real, don't they?"

"Practically are," Chancy said. "They bit me many a time." He picked up his hat and the handles of the wheelbarrow. "If you follow me one more step, I'll take those grinders away from you."

He headed back into the sun. He was almost afraid to glance over his shoulder, but when he did Jody was clacking the teeth and heading for home. Chancy began to whistle again. He felt suddenly that he had outgrown those scary old teeth anyway. He was glad to let Jody have them.

Two days later he met a one-eyed man.

2

Colonel Plugg

THE MAN was sitting on a butternut stump at the crossroad. He wore a leather eye patch, a tail coat and a double gold watch chain across his vest. He was fanning his plump red face with a beaver hat when Chancy came whistling along. At the man's feet stood a straw suitcase.

"How do, boy?"

Chancy had never met a man with an eye patch and it gave him a start. He had hardly come thirty miles and the world was starting to shower its wonders on him. "Howdy, sir."

"By Jacks, you come along like an angel of mercy. Stay a moment. Colonel Plugg's my name. *Ahem*. You're heading over to Tulip Tree, I fancy. You can do me a large favor. *Ahem*. You've heard of me, of course."

"No, sir," Chancy said. The eye patch was as fascinating as a loose tooth, and he could hardly keep from staring at it. "I'm a stranger down this way."

"Well, that explains it," the man laughed. "Everybody knows me in these parts. I do a bit of scientific farming, you might say. That hundred and sixty acres back yonder, where you see the house — that belongs to me. Judge Coatjohn's

place, it used to be. I planted it in nutmegs. Imported the
seed all the way from the East Indies. The whole thing's
scientific. *Ahem.* Ain't another nutmeg plantation in the
country." He wiped out his wing collar with a linen handkerchief. "It'll be worth untold millions when it comes into
bearing, I can tell you."

Chancy tried to keep his attention focused on the man's
good eye, which was a piercing blue. Colonel Plugg was

clearly an important person. True, his beaver hat looked a bit mangy, but he carried a white linen handkerchief and it wasn't even Sunday. Chancy was impressed.

"I was just marching to Tulip Tree myself," said Colonel Plugg, "but I don't mind telling you my leg ain't what it used to be before the war. Stopped a musket ball at Vicksburg. *Ahem*. Left knee. The ball's still in there. By Jacks, that wheelbarrow is a handy contrivance, boy. What do you say I just pile on my suitcase and we'll walk along together."

Chancy's ears had pricked up. Vicksburg! His father had fought at Vicksburg. Chancy found a place for the suitcase. "Maybe you knew my father," he said. "Dr. Rufus Dundee. He was at Vicksburg, too."

"I declare!" Colonel Plugg began loping along beside him, favoring his left knee. "Dundee, you say. Dundee. No, I don't seem to recollect that name. *Ahem*. There was a right smart lot of us, you know. I tell you, the musket balls were flying about like hornets. Had two horses shot out from under me, poor beasts. No, I don't believe I knew your father."

Chancy was disappointed, but he was glad to have Colonel Plugg along. The man hardly stopped talking. It passed the time and Chancy listened attentively. He didn't mind the extra load on his wheelbarrow. But when he bounced the wheel over a rut the colonel was quick to caution him.

"Easy with that suitcase, boy. It's full of eggs."

"Eggs?"

"Five dozen of the largest, freshest eggs you ever saw. They're still warm from the hens. And all triple-yolkers."

"Triple-yolkers, sir?"

"I guarantee it. I keep a few prime chickens, you know, and raise 'em scientific. Three yolks to every shell. Folks call 'em Colonel Plugg's Ohio Wonder Eggs. The general store at Tulip Tree is always trying to buy my triple-yolkers, but they ain't for sale, usually. *Ahem.* Prefer to give them away to the poor. But if I don't exercise my leg the Doc says it'll go lame on me, so I thought I'd march down to the store and sell a few eggs."

Chancy was curious to see one of the wonder eggs. He avoided every bump in the road. He couldn't very well expect Colonel Plugg to take a turn at the wheelbarrow, not with a musket ball in his knee.

"How far you wayfarin', boy?"

"Paducah, sir," Chancy said. "Aim to catch the steamboat."

"Fine place, Paducah. Been there many a-time myself. You must look up my old friend Colonel Shrewsbury and extend my compliments. *Ahem.* But see here, if you're taking the steamboat you must have the fare money in your pocket. All varieties of scamps and rascals along the river. Cut your throat for a dollar or less. You be careful, boy. Take my word and never trust a man in a slouch hat. I never met a man in a slouch hat who didn't have five aces up his sleeve. A bad lot, I'll tell you. They'd steal the bark off a tree. When you get down to the river, keep an eye peeled for slouch hats and hide your money. I'm telling you this for your own good."

"Much obliged," Chancy said. It struck him as a quirkish sort of warning, but he felt he ought to take all the advice he could get. And he did have a three-dollar gold piece in a pouch around his neck. It had taken him years to save it. Once he reached the river, he'd keep an eye peeled.

It was surprising how quickly Colonel Plugg strode along, even with a musket ball in his knee. Chancy could hardly keep up. Then, with Tulip Tree almost in sight, the colonel's leg almost went out from under him.

"Hold it, boy. I'll be blessed if I can go another step. My knee has plumb give out. Help me yonder into the shade. Thank you. Thank you, boy."

Chancy half-supported him to a large buckeye and the old soldier eased himself to the ground with his back against the trunk. Chancy regarded him anxiously. A wounded man oughten to be out walking in the hot sun, no sir.

Colonel Plugg mopped his face with the handkerchief. "By Jacks, that musket ball feels as swelled up as a cannon-ball in my knee. Reckon I overdid the marching. I'm stuck here, it looks like. *Ahem.* May have to sit the rest of the day before the swelling goes down."

"I'm desperate sorry," said Chancy.

"No matter. None at all. But you'd be doing me a large favor to take those eggs to the store while they're still fresh. If it wouldn't be too much trouble."

"None at all."

"Thank you, boy. Chancy was your name, wasn't it?"

"Yes, sir."

"Let me see, them triple-yolkers ought to fetch nine cents each. The five dozen would come to five-forty. You just say they're Colonel Plugg's Ohio Wonder Eggs and there'll be no trouble about the price. I aim to reward you with a dollar, Chancy, if you wouldn't mind bringing me back the proceeds. Town's just the other side of that hill."

"A dollar!"

"That's what I said."

Chancy was dazzled by his sudden good luck. The buckeye in his hip pocket must be working. A dollar was a bountiful sum and he was eager to earn it.

"You rest easy, sir," he said. "By dogs, I'll have your egg money back in no time. No time at all."

"I'll just wait here in the shade and ease my leg." The colonel fanned his flushed face with the beaver hat. "But see here, Chancy, we ought to do this businesslike and scientific. Not that you don't have an honest face. I know you ain't going to skedaddle with my egg money. Bless you, the thought hasn't entered your head — I can see that."

Chancy gave him a guarded look. "No sir."

"Don't take offense," Colonel Plugg said quickly. "But I'd hate to be the cause of putting temptation in a lad's path. By Jacks, that would weigh on my conscience every minute you was gone. Not that temptation could stand up to a hard-working, open-hearted youngster such as yourself. Not likely. But the thing to do is go by the book. *Ahem.* And the book says a chunk of security is called for in a case like this."

"Security?" Chancy said. He began to feel uneasy. Earning that dollar was getting complicated.

"The party of the *first* part — that's you, Chancy — puts up some trifling item of value. The party of the *second* part — that's me — I hold it until you get back with the egg money. That's the businesslike thing to do, fair and square. A boy can't learn the ways of good business too early in life."

Chancy took a breath. "If that's what the book says," he nodded. The suspicion that he might run off ruffled him, but he could see Colonel Plugg's side of it. Chancy was only a stranger to him. And with his leg as stiff as a slat, the man was rooted to the spot. He'd be helpless if Chancy skedaddled. "I could leave my shoes behind," he said.

"Well, no. I never met a boy who'd come back for his shoes. Say you was to put up your axe. *Ahem.* I doubt if it's equal to the value of my straw suitcase — not to mention the eggs at all. But I'd accept the axe. You'll get it back, of course. We're just going by the book."

"No, sir," Chancy said firmly. "I reckon I don't want to put up my Pa's axe. If that's what the book says I guess not. I won't be earning that dollar."

"Hold on. Of course you won't part from the axe, it be-ing your own father's, like you just said. Well, that's why they invented cash money. You just put up five dollars. Climb this old buckeye and leave it on a high branch where I can't touch it. It'll be there when you get back. Mind, it's just the principle of the thing I'm trying to learn you."

"Yes, sir," Chancy said. "But I don't have five dollars."

"Four?"

"Three." Chancy wished suddenly he were shed of Colonel Plugg and his triple-yolk eggs. And yet, what did he have to fear? With his bad leg the colonel couldn't climb the tree if the ground were afire. "That's all the cash money I own. It's my steamboat fare."

"Done!" said Colonel Plugg. "I'm getting the short end of the security — you understand that. But I won't quibble. Done, I say. When you get back you'll have an extra dollar for your trouble. *Ahem.* I don't mind telling you you'll need it. Steamboat fare to Paducah'll run you all of four dollars."

If what Colonel Plugg said was true, the extra dollar loomed with special importance. Chancy hesitated only another moment. He hated to part with his gold piece, but he'd soon be back for it. He pulled the leather pouch from around his neck, climbed the tree and hung it on a branch. He slid to the ground and picked up the wheelbarrow. "I'll be back."

"I'll be waiting."

Chancy went trundling down the road. The village wasn't just beyond the hill. It was across a dry creek and through a cornfield and the other side of a magnolia standing as huge as a thunderhead. It was almost half an hour before Chancy reached his destination. The village seemed composed of little more than the big tulip tree and Pickawilly's General Mercantile & Feed Store.

Chancy helped himself at the water barrel on the porch. A lanky man with shiny black sleeve guards and a turkey feather duster sticking out of his hip pocket came through the door and began to hang fresh curls of flypaper. "Hot enough for you?" he smiled.

"Yes, sir," Chancy said emphatically. "I'm about to melt out of my clothes. Are you Mr. Pickawilly?"

The storekeeper nodded. "Anything I can do for you?"

"Colonel Plugg sent me with these eggs to sell you."

"I can use some eggs. They fresh?"

"Yes, sir. Still warm from the hen." Chancy threw back the lid and exposed the eggs to the sun. "Five dozen of Colonel Plugg's Ohio Wonder Eggs. Triple-yolkers, you know."

"*Triple*-yolkers?"

"Guaranteed."

"Well, that's a new one on me." The storekeeper gazed at the mixed brown and white eggs. "Kind of chalky-looking, some of 'em. What you asking?"

"Nine cents each."

"Each!"

"They're wonder eggs. Raised scientific, you know."

It seemed peculiar to Chancy that the storekeeper didn't already know about Colonel Plugg's triple-yolk eggs. And then Chancy heard a faint pecking sound from the suitcase. A white egg was twitching. Chancy gazed at it unbelieving. Another began to rock. And then, before his eyes, a shell broke and a wet chick began to chirp.

Chancy was thunderstruck. Mr. Pickawilly straightened and shook his head. "Young feller, those eggs are about as fresh as last summer's calendar. The sun's hatching 'em out."

"But, sir — "

The whole top layer was beginning to rock about in the straw packing. The storekeeper regarded Chancy thoughtfully. "Who did you say sent you?"

"Colonel Plugg."

"He live around here?"

"Yes, sir. He owns Judge Coatjohn's old place. Planted it in nutmeg trees."

"Nutmegs! Why, boy, you can't grow nutmegs around

here or anywhere else I know of. I've never heard of a Judge Coatjohn, either, and I've lived here all my life. Did that man sell you these stale eggs?"

Chancy felt his face redden. "No, sir. But I did have to leave my three-dollar gold piece behind. We went by the book. Security, he called it."

"You'd better hurry back and get it, son. If he ain't up and gone already."

Chancy found some hope to cling to. "I reckon he's still resting in the shade. He's laid up with a musket ball in his knee."

"Musket ball! I wager there's nothing wrong with his

knee. You've been fast-talked, boy. I hate to tell you that. This time of year brings out a regiment of wayfarers and whatnot. Sell you the blue sky overhead even on a cloudy day. That swindler is long gone by now. But I'll hitch up the buggy and we'll go see. I'd mighty like to see you get your money back." Mr. Pickawilly turned and called through the screen door. "Old lady! You watch the store. I'll be back."

Colonel Plugg was gone. Chancy peered up into the branches of the buckeye tree. His heart felt as heavy as a grindstone. The money pouch was no longer hanging from the limb, but he climbed the tree anyway and looked all around. It couldn't be true, but it was. His three-dollar gold piece was gone.

"You might as well come down," the storekeeper called. "Frettin' won't get your money back."

Chancy wiped the sweat off his face in the crook of his sleeve. He lingered another moment and then lowered himself to the ground. He was too old to cry. And anyway, Mr. Pickawilly was looking at him.

Chancy took a long breath and climbed into the buggy. The storekeeper turned back in the direction of Tulip Tree. "One of them river scamps, mostly likely," he said. "There are more colonels along the river these days than fought the war, both sides. And wore an eye patch, did he! Oh, he's a cunning one. Reckon his two eyes are as lively as his two legs. He's probably in the state of Indiana by now!"

Chancy clamped his jaws. He didn't have sense enough to pull in his head when he shut the window. He'd been humbugged every step of the way. No wonder Colonel

Plugg had hurried him along the road. He wanted to be shed of those stale eggs before they hatched. Well, if that scoundrel ever crossed his path again he'd be sorry. Tarnation, he would!

"You come along back and stay for supper," said Mr. Pickawilly. "We'll fix you a place to sleep. I don't usually buy day-old chicks, but I'll give you a penny apiece for those that hatch."

Chancy looked up gratefully. But now Paducah seemed a long way off. It might take him most of the summer by foot. He dug the buckeye out of his pocket and glared at it. A precious lot of good luck that had brought him. He wanted to hurl it to the road, but held back. He was afraid. Throwing away a good luck piece seemed an awful act; it might let loose all its dark powers against him. In the end he tucked it back into his hip pocket. He'd give it one more chance.

3

The Coming-and-Going Man

THE EGGS were hatching like popcorn in the suitcase. By morning Chancy counted eighteen chicks, and more to come. But he wanted to be on his way and decided to take the remaining eggs with him. One huge brown one had caught his eye and he was curious to see the chick that hatched out of it. He might be able to peddle the newborn chicks along the way.

"I'll split you some cook wood for my meals and lodging," he said. "I'm tolerably handy with an axe."

"Got plenty, thanks just the same." Mr. Pickawilly smiled, pulling on his sleeve guards. "But that gives me an idea. When you get to the river you stack some firewood on the bank. Lay up six, eight cords if your back holds out. One of them steamboats'll stop and buy it off you. Bound to. They burn up a smart lot of wood, you know. Hardly carry a half-day supply, most of them. There's woodyards all along the river, and no reason you can't make yourself steamboat fare and then some. How does that strike you?"

Chancy's eyebrows lifted at the possibilities. "By dogs!"

"Chop the wood four foot long. And you charge a dollar-fifty a cord, hear?"

"Yes, sir." Chancy was dazzled. He now saw a fortune waiting for him. Why, he'd chop a hill of wood. An almighty mountain of wood. And if he could sell his poultry along the way, he'd arrive in Paducah weighted down with cash money.

Mr. Pickawilly paid him for the chicks and weighed up a sack of mash. The chicks that hatched on the road would have to be fed. Chancy found a place in the wheelbarrow for the mash and filled his cider jug with fresh water. Then he ran back his lanky hair and pulled on his hat. "Thank you, sir. Thank you for everything."

"Good luck. And here — I cut you a piece of bacon rind to grease that wheel. It squeaks something terrible."

A moment later Chancy was strutting down the road. He turned and gave Mr. Pickawilly a final wave. He was feeling downright light-hearted again.

Six more chicks hatched during the heat of the day. Chancy punched holes in the straw suitcase for air and stopped now and then to turn the eggs. None of the brown ones had yet hatched. It seemed a wonder to him that any of the eggs had hatched without the hen to keep turning them, and to keep them warm. Well, the days were hot enough and the nights too. And he supposed the eggs had been upended often enough as they traveled about in the suitcase.

The six chicks kept chirping and peeping, and it was like having a small orchestra along. He fixed a gourd of water in the suitcase and continued on his way. He offered the chicks for sale to passersby, but when night fell he still had the six left. It would be easier to sell fleas to a dog, he thought. The farmers had poultry of their own they'd be glad to sell him.

He slept that night in a cornfield and reached the river late the following morning.

He could smell it first, something fresh and heavy in the air. Then he got a shimmering glimpse through the woods. Finally he trundled the wheelbarrow through a tangle of high-water debris, across a dry and cracked mud flat, and didn't stop until he was ankle deep in the Ohio River. He gave a whoop and a holler, and wished Jody could be here to see it for himself.

It was the grandest sight he could recall. The river stretched a quarter of a mile wide and so sparkling in the sun that it might have been covered with fish scales. That would be Kentucky at the other bank, and it seemed uncanny to stand in the state of Ohio and look at the state of Kentucky. The river was low — easy moving and hardly bothering to make any sound at all. For a moment nothing stirred but a dragonfly chasing about in the sun. Chancy gazed at the Ohio and felt like some great trailblazer who had just discovered it.

Chancy followed a bend in the river to the shade of an overhanging swamp willow and shoved the wheelbarrow out of sight in a tall bristle of cattails. Then he shucked his clothes and took a leap. The cold water hit him like the kick of a mule, but it felt splendid. He pushed aside a sumpy log and found himself in the water with a ninety-pound catfish. The catfish, brown as mud, left in a hurry.

Chancy broke off a willow twig, chewed the end until it was frayed and brushed his teeth. He was filled with a wondrous sense of achievement. He had reached the Ohio. He was swimming in it. Paducah was somewhere downriver and he'd get there too. He'd find Indiana. And maybe she'd know where to start looking for Mirandy and little Jamie.

But Paducah would have to wait while he stacked up cord wood. He looked with calculating eyes at the fallen trees and uprooted stumps tossed high and dry by old flood waters. It was his for the gathering and the chopping. In his mind the woodyard grew to magnificent proportions.

He was eager to get started. He was pulling his shirt over his head when he thought he heard a sound in the distance. A moment later he saw a man sauntering around the bend. Chancy gave a start. The approaching stranger was wearing a slouch hat.

Chancy dropped down among the cattails and held his breath. The river abounded with scoundrels this time of year, didn't it? Even Mr. Pickawilly had warned him about that. Slowly parting the cattails Chancy watched as the man came tramping along the dry bank above. His boots were scuffed and dusty. He was huge and broad-shouldered with a rolled army blanket slung across his back. A thin black cigar, crooked as a twig, was locked between his teeth. A bounder for sure, Chancy thought. He carried a tattered carpetbag in each hand. His coat flapped with every step and his yellow calico vest shone in the sun.

Chancy became aware of the faint chirps and squeaks from the suitcase beside him. His breath caught. The chicks would give away his hiding place. And then the man stopped.

His sharp eyes seemed to range over the cattails. Chancy didn't move. The chicks were peeping away merrily.

Chancy began to edge closer to the handle of his Pa's four-pound axe. That stranger had better keep his distance.

Then the summer stillness was broken by the blast of a steam whistle. A riverboat loaded with mules came huffing and clanking around the bend. The stern wheel kicked up a waterfall and the sound of the chicks was drowned out. The stranger gave a shrug and continued on his way.

Chancy waited. The wash of the steamboat reached the cattails and started them swaying and rustling. Chancy peered at the stern-wheeler. How it strutted! And how he wished he were aboard, making for Paducah.

When the stranger was well out of sight downriver, Chancy picked up the wheelbarrow and headed upriver. That man was looking for mischief, he thought. He might have tried to make off with the four-pound axe. Chancy felt well rid of him.

When he had gone almost a mile he stopped to gaze at an island standing out of the river like a turtle shell. He meant to pick the spot for his woodyard carefully. It was a fat little island with shady willows growing as rank as weeds. That might do. That might do fine. He could see a litter of snag wood and fallen trees to start on. By dogs, that was the place for his woodyard.

He rolled up his trouser legs and shoved the wheelbarrow into the shallow channel. He was careful not to capsize the chicks, the eggs and his belongings. A moment later he took possession of the island. There was no one to greet him but five crows flocked on the roots of an overturned tree stump. They clapped their black wings and flew off cawing to Kentucky across the river.

Chancy had never been on an island before. He dug his

feet in the warm earth and surveyed his small domain. He wondered if it had a name. Probably not, he thought. It was just a trifling island, he imagined — maybe no man had ever set foot there before. He liked the thought. He folded his arms and decided to name the place Crow Island.

Within twenty minutes he had every foot of the island explored. He found a broken oar, a tar bucket with some tar still in it, the arm of a chair and half a red barn door. Best of all he found a patch of watermelon vines growing wild at the lower end of the island. He picked out the ripest melon and split it open with his axe. He let the chicks on the ground, cut them a chunk to peck at and settled himself in the shade to eat.

After a while he got up and turned the brown eggs. He wondered if they were ever going to hatch. Especially that huge one. But after they hatched what in tarnation would he do with them? No fancy steamboat was going to pull up to Crow Island and ask to buy his poultry. And he couldn't turn them loose — chicken hawks would get them for sure.

He watched them clustered at the melon rind, squeaking away like a flock of hinges. Now that they were two days old they were beginning to eat. It was a peck of trouble having chicks along, but they were good company. He didn't feel entirely alone with something live and friendly chasing around his feet. With the days and nights so hot they didn't need a brooder to keep warm. But he couldn't have them underfoot when he began felling trees. He'd better coop them.

He laid out four dead limbs in the shape of a box and plugged the chinks with dirt. That would do fine. He lifted the chicks one by one and set them inside. They rolled off his hand like yellow balls of sunlight. He fixed the water gourd in a corner and scattered a handful of mash.

Then he unloaded the wheelbarrow and chose the spot for his woodyard. He'd build it on the river side of the island so that the steamboats could see it. He started out with the wheelbarrow and returned with a load of driftwood. By late afternoon he had gathered most of the dead limbs and snag wood to be found on the island. He chopped the longer pieces into four-foot lengths and began stacking. By nightfall he had better than half a cord laid up. When he finished he stood back in a glow of sweat and looked it over with satisfaction. His woodyard was under way.

Nearby, he propped the slab of barn door against two stumps. It made a fine shelter.

Sometime during mid-morning the brown eggs began to hatch.

Chancy had busied himself with a spindly, lightning-struck willow. The trunk was hardly as thick as stovepipe. He'd felled it, stripped the branches and chopped it into lengths. He was hauling them to the woodpile when he noticed three red chicks flitting around the coop. They had already dried off and found their legs.

"Well, howdy!" he grinned.

He sat on his haunches and watched the goings-on. The new chicks gave him darting glances with their black, buckshot eyes. He could hear the *tap-tap-tap* of other chicks pecking away inside their shells. Soon the top of an egg broke away and Chancy could see the wet, scrawny chick inside. It fell back exhausted. But soon it began struggling out of the shell; it kicked and scratched, half in and half out. Finally it was free. Then it went stumbling about, unable to master its pinkish legs. It rested and tried again.

Chancy stood up. Before long it would be rushing around with the others, and watching wouldn't get his wood stacked. And the big brown egg hadn't yet hatched. That was the one he was waiting for. He got back to work. When he finished with the spindly willow there were eleven newborn chicks in the coop.

He stopped long enough to eat and put an edge on the axe with his small whetstone. He was getting quite a flock, and didn't they chirp and chitter! He suddenly remembered a long time ago when his father had brought home a Shanghai rooster. It had pecked at everyone's legs and chased his sister Indiana half a mile down the road. They had had to get rid of it.

Chancy picked out a branchy tree not far off at the edge of the island. He calculated he could get half a cord out of that tree, limbs and all.

The axe rang out. He stopped now and then to spit on his hands. It might take him the rest of the month to lay up six or eight cords, but every bite of the axe edged him closer to Paducah. Finally, when he had the tree almost balanced to fall, he looked up and saw a man standing fifteen feet away. He was thunderstruck.

It was the wide-shouldered man in the dark slouch hat.

Chancy tried not to betray his surprise. It wouldn't do to let this man see that he was scared. "Nice day," he said.

"Fine day." The man was peering at him with squinted green eyes. A smile spread around the cigar clamped be-

tween his teeth. He put down his two carpetbags and un-
shouldered his bedroll.

Chancy didn't trust the man's smile. "I wouldn't stand
that close, sir," he said. "This big ol' tree is fixing to fall."

"Big?" the man laughed. "Why, Chancy, I generally pull
small trees like that up by the roots."

Chancy! How had this river vagabond learned his name?
From Colonel Plugg, most likely. *That* scoundrel must
have told him about the fine four-pound axe Chancy had
along.

Chancy's muscles tightened and he watched for any sudden movement. The wing feather of a hawk was tucked in
the man's hatband. His boots were dripping wet; he had
come wading across to the island. "I declare," he said,

studying Chancy closely. "You don't look like you been getting enough to eat, boy. It wouldn't hurt to fatten you up. You could take a bath in a shotgun barrel."

"I got along plenty to eat," Chancy answered defiantly, and was immediately sorry he had admitted it.

"Splendid!" the stranger laughed, and the hawk's feather quivered in his hat. "I'm hungry. You've been as hard to catch as a squirrel. I don't mind telling you that."

"I'm not caught yet, sir." Chancy didn't move from the tree trunk. A mere push and the willow would go crashing down. That man would find himself driven into the ground like a stake. "Don't come any closer."

The man chuckled. "You're mighty skittish about strangers. I can see that. But you wouldn't turn away a hungry man, would you? And we're not purely strangers — not if your name's Chancy B. Dundee."

"No, sir, it ain't. You just missed him. He's heading up-river to Cincinnati, I believe. If you hurry, you might actually catch up."

"We're not strangers," the man went on. "Not if you left Squire Starbuck's place five days ago. Not if you've got a sister Indiana and a brother Jamie and a sister Mirandy. And *not* if the B in your name stands for Buckthorn—after your Ma's side of the family."

Chancy felt his eyes go as hard as oak knots. He was stunned. This was far more than he had told Colonel Plugg.

"Tarnation, who are you, sir!"

"Me?" The man laughed and the hawk's feather quivered again. "Why, Chancy, I'm a coming-and-going man, that's who I am! I can shoe a runaway horse and out-calculate a pack of foxes. I'm half fox myself, and the other half prairie buffalo! I'm a wayfaring printer, mule skinner, soldier, tinkerer, Indian fighter, barn painter and everything in between. I've been clear to California and I once pulled a wagon with my teeth. If that don't suit you, why, I can out-laugh, out-exaggerate and out-rascal any man this side of the Big Muddy, and twice as many on the other! Look at these eyes of mine. Cat's eyes, same as yours! Didn't they tell you there was a grand rascal in the family, Chancy? Didn't they tell you about your wanderin', fiddle-footed uncle? Your darlin' mother's own brother! By the eternal, boy! Drop that axe and come say howdy to your uncle — Will Buckthorn!"

4
Will Buckthorn

WHAT IT WAS that made the willow choose that moment to fall Chancy didn't know. But the tree cracked like a chicken bone. Chancy didn't have time to say howdy. He shouted, "Run!"

The tree came roaring down and bounced in a shower of leaves. Chancy's breath stopped short. When the air cleared, Will Buckthorn had vanished.

Chancy dropped the axe and leaped forward. "Sir! Uncle Will!"

"By the eternal!" answered Will Buckthorn, stepping from behind a nearby tree and looking around for his hat. "That's not the friendliest welcome I ever had, Chancy, but it was the windiest."

A smile shot to Chancy's eyes. He remembered wondrous stories his mother used to tell about her brother Will. And there he stood! This big, curly-haired stranger was his kin. It seemed too marvelous to believe. Chancy found the slouch hat under a branch and began dusting it off. "Howdy, Uncle Will." And then he added, "I'm infernal sorry about that tree."

Will Buckthorn studied him carefully. "Chancy, I'd shake your hand if I knew for certain you didn't have a bolt of lightning up your sleeve."

"No sir, I don't."

Uncle Will put out his hand. They shook and gazed at each other and grinned. "Let me take a good look at you," said Will Buckthorn. "You're growing up to look like your Pa, I can see that. He had hair straight as wheat straw and you got his nose, sharp as an axe. And you smile like him, too."

"I declare." Chancy was glad to hear that. He handed back the hat.

"But those specks on your eyes you got from your Ma. Cat's eyes run in our family, you know."

Chancy could see Uncle Will's own cat's eyes. He felt a glow of pride and kinship. To think that he had almost dropped a tree on him! He wondered now how he could have been spooked by the slouch hat. He should have known better than to take Colonel Plugg's word for anything.

Will Buckthorn's voice softened. "I was almighty slow finding out about your Pa and Ma, Chancy. I'm desperate sorry."

Chancy nodded. "We figured you'd been lost in the war or got scalped by Indians. Miss Russell — she was our neighbor — she wrote you letters, but they all came back."

"I must have been livin' among the Comanches about then, and those folks don't have a mail delivery. You young'uns are the only kin I got left. If I'd known you had been left alone, I'd have escaped quicker."

"Comanches!" Chancy murmured in awe.

"It wasn't until a few months ago that I got back to Erie County and found all you Dundees split up."

"Mirandy and little Jamie, too?" Chancy asked. He hadn't had any news of them in four years. He'd hoped they might have stayed put, but it wouldn't surprise him if they had been taken a thousand miles away. "Aren't they still with Miss Russell?"

"She's gone too, and never heard from. I don't mind telling you I been all over the Ohio map picking up your tracks. Traced you to Sandusky. Missed you at Squire Starbuck's. Missed you at Pickawilly's store. You weren't hard to follow, though. A regiment of folks saw you along the road with your wheelbarrow and chicks. Thought I'd about caught up to you at the river, but I headed downriver and you headed up. Finally backtrailed it this way and heard you whacking at a tree. But by ginger, I caught up to you at last!"

Chancy grinned. "I didn't know anybody was looking for me."

"You laying up wood for the winter?"

"No, sir. I'm starting a woodyard."

Uncle Will shoved back his hat. "A woodyard?"

"I figure on earning steamboat fare to Paducah," Chancy said. "That's where they took my sister Indiana. I aim to hunt her up."

Uncle Will's face changed, like the sun slipping out of the clouds. "Splendid! See here, I'm handy with a chopping axe. We'll put up your woodpile quicker'n a frog can clear his throat. I'm short of steamboat fare myself. I'd like to come along to Paducah with you, if you wouldn't mind my company."

"Mind!" Chancy's eyes lit up. "By dogs, I'd *like* to have you along, Uncle Will. Reckon so. Won't Indiana be surprised when we walk in, you and me! And then maybe we could set out for Mirandy and Jamie."

"Maybe?" Will Buckthorn's laughter boomed out again. "We'll track 'em down if it takes from July to eternity!"

Chancy fetched Uncle Will's bedroll and two carpetbags and showed off his chicks and his woodpile. Before long Uncle Will hung his coat on a limb, borrowed Chancy's axe, and all that afternoon the chips flew like great wet sparks. He'd set his eye on a tree, fell it, spit to one side, strip the limbs and hardly work up a sweat. Chancy's admiration was unbounded.

He could hardly drag wood to the pile fast enough to keep up. He had become aware of a muffled sound from one of the carpetbags; it seemed to him a dozen somethings going clickety-click. His eye kept straying to it throughout the afternoon. But he figured it was none of his business and didn't want to ask about it.

By sundown the woodpile had risen like bread in an oven and Uncle Will looked it over with satisfaction. "Splendid," he said. "You're stacking the wood good and tight. I've known grown men to lay up cords so loose you could hold a cat fight inside. You can tell a man's character by lookin' at his firewood. Yes sir, that's a fine woodpile, Chancy."

Chancy was eager for Uncle Will's approval. Tomorrow he'd stack the lengths even tighter. They'd have the best woodyard on the river.

They ate, sitting against a tree, and watched night come

to the Ohio. Chancy already felt that he had known Uncle Will all his life. The air began to sing with bugs and insects. Finally Uncle Will lit one of his twisted black cigars and Chancy got out his buckeye to polish it. By dogs, there was a power in it, he thought. To think he had almost pitched it away! Colonel Plugg had been bad luck, but there sat Uncle Will beside him — yes sir, there was a power in the buckeye after all. "You calculate Indiana will know what happened to Mirandy and little Jamie?" he asked.

"Oh, I know where to begin looking for them," Uncle Will said, and Chancy's ears pricked up. "They're somewhere out on the Great Plains."

"The Great Plains!" Chancy was stunned. The far prairies west of the Mississippi seemed as remote as the dark side of the moon. "Tarnation."

Uncle Will pulled off his boots. "That's where we'll find them, near as I could find out. Your neighbor lady, Miss Russell, kept the little ones together in Erie County, bless

her young heart. But it appears some gentleman was writing her letters and asked to marry her, sight unseen. I reckon she wanted to make a real home for the young'uns. She packed 'em up and lit out West. That was more'n a year ago. That gentleman is a big cattleman I was told, but no one could recollect his name or where he did his ranchin'. Mirandy and little Jamie could be livin' anywhere from Texas to Montana, but we'll pick up their trail somehow. I've walked every foot of that country."

Chancy felt a flash of hope. With Uncle Will along the world already seemed a smaller place. Why, once they reached the Great Plains he could probably whistle loud enough to bring Mirandy and little Jamie running.

Again Chancy's eye strayed to the carpetbag rattling away inside, clickety-click. "How did you escape from the Comanches, Uncle Will?"

"I didn't escape exactly. Who told you that?"

"You did, sir."

"I declare. Then it must be so. I thought I was rescued."

"Who rescued you?"

"A big bull buffalo."

"A buffalo!" Chancy exclaimed.

Uncle Will laughed. "I do exaggerate occasionally — but that's the solemn truth, Chancy. Remind me sometime and I'll tell you about the winter I lived on tree bark. But about those Comanches. After the war some of us horse soldiers were sent out to fight the plains Indians. I got ambushed. Those Comanches didn't know what to do with me. I was too big for a man and too small for a buffalo. You can see that."

"Yes, sir."

"Those Indians kept me along with them for two years. I near turned into a Comanche myself."

"Is that when you lived on tree bark?"

"No. We were trailing near the Wyoming border, near as I can figure, when a buffalo stampede came down on us. My horse got tired of me in a hurry and pitched me into the air. The buffalo were so thick around us you couldn't see the ground. I landed on the hide of a big bull buffalo."

Chancy was all ears.

"He tried to buck me off, but I had no intention of leavin' his company. I dug my hands into the shaggy fur at his shoulders and held on tighter than a new boot. He plunged around, snorting fire, and the next thing I knew he broke away from the herd and went rattling out across the prairie lickety-whoop. Chancy, it was like hangin' onto the wind itself. Didn't he take me for a ride, though! It was tremendous. When he finally got winded and slowed to a walk I slipped off his rump and thanked him as best I

could. The Comanches were miles out of sight. To this day I believe they're still wonderin' what happened to me."

Chancy basked in the glow of Uncle Will's adventures. He was enchanted. "Is that when you had to live on tree bark?"

"Well, no." And here a different light came into Will Buckthorn's eyes. "That was the following winter up in Dakota when I got snowed in. I had nothing to eat but my belt and my boots. They don't taste half bad, boiled. After that there was nothing to do but start in on the tree bark. There are places up in that country where it's twenty miles between trees, but I was lucky. I had all the aspens I could eat, and some bur oak too. I didn't go hungry. Chancy, you won't believe it, but when spring came along I'd eaten so much wood that the sap began to rise in my veins — and I broke into bud. That's the almighty truth! And that's not even the worst of it. For three months after that I couldn't scratch my back without givin' myself splinters!"

Chancy, after almost swallowing the story whole, now burst into a laugh and Uncle Will roared. Their voices carried out across the water. Later, they made up beds of leaves and laid out their blankets. The chicks were huddled together with heads tucked under their wings. Stars swarmed overhead and a bullfrog began to croak.

Then Uncle Will opened the noisy carpetbag. He lifted out a clock. And then another. The bag was almost full of clocks, and all of them rattling away like woodpeckers.

"You a clock seller, Uncle Will?"

"Forced into it." He began to wind each clock with a brass key. "I met up with a Connecticut clock peddler in a train depot a few weeks back. I had my tinker's kit and some old socks in a carpetbag. He picked it up by mistake and left me this one. It made a clock peddler out of me and I reckon a tinkerer out of him. Of course, he got the best of it. He's got them spare socks. These clocks are about as easy to sell as toothpicks to a catfish. You'd be surprised how many folks don't give a hang what time it is. I think that Yankee changed bags with me a-purpose."

"What time is it, Uncle Will?"

"Don't know. One of these is bound to tell the right time, but I'll be shot if I know which one it is."

Day by day the woodpile grew and the hatching came to an end. Chancy had fourteen eggs left over, which he put aside to bury. The huge brown egg was among them, unhatched, and he was disappointed. In the summer heat they were no doubt going rotten and he'd better bury them before one broke and raised a smell. Still, he waited.

It was late the following day when he made up his mind to be done with it. And that's when he saw an eggshell split open. It was empty.

By dogs! The big brown one had hatched!

He looked all around for the chick. He fell to his hands and knees to search in the twilight through the tall grass. He listened for a peeping sound, and soon Uncle Will joined in the hunt.

"That chick couldn't be more than a few hours old and he's already out seeing the world," Chancy grinned.

It was soon dark. "Better let it go till daylight," Uncle Will said. "We might step on him."

"I do want that chick," Chancy said.

"We'll turn him up before breakfast. Glory be, from the size of that shell he must have hatched full-grown!"

5

Calamity

WHEN CHANCY awoke he saw a chicken hawk like a spot before his eyes in the dawn sky.

He leaped from his blanket and hurried to the week-old chicks scratching around in the open coop. He herded the flock to safety under the straw suitcase. The hawk, its wings fanned like outstretched claws, began circling overhead.

Uncle Will was watching him too. After a moment he said, "That varmint's got his eye on other game. Chancy, he's spied out your lost peep."

Chancy picked up a handful of stones. The soaring hawk was tightening its circles and drifting over the lower end of the island.

Chancy began to run. He tried to keep one eye on the hawk and the other on the ground.

"Chick, chick!" he called. Where was that pesky chick? Didn't he have better sense than to go meandering off by himself? That infernal hawk would get him for sure. "Chick, chick!"

Suddenly Chancy saw the hawk drop from the sky. Uncle Will began waving his coat in the air. *"Kee-aah! Kee-aah!"*

he yelled. Chancy hurried along in a blind fury. Where was that fool chick!

"Chick, chick!"

"*Kee-aah! Kee-aah!*"

From a tangle of debris ahead Chancy heard a muffled *cheep-cheep-cheep-cheep*. At almost the same instant he saw the hawk swoop down for the kill. It's tail fanned, its wings thrashed the air — and its talons struck at an old fallen log.

"*Kee-aah! Kee-aah!*" Chancy shouted, and fired the stones like buckshot. The hawk gave out a great angry squawk and flapped its huge wings. Then it swept out over the water. Its talons were empty. Chancy heaved another handful of stones and rushed to the log. It was hollow. He dropped to his knees and peered inside. He could see a pair of shining eyes deep within. The chick was screeching away furiously.

"Uncle Will! Look here!"

He reached inside, but the chick backed deeper into the

hollow. Finally Uncle Will lifted one end of the log and the chick came tumbling out like a ball of fire. Chancy caught hold of him. The chick was a foxy red and as light as air. He took a peck at Chancy's fingers.

"That's the maddest peep I ever saw," Uncle Will laughed.

"And the biggest! Must be a rooster."

"He's big, all right. I do believe that hawk got off lucky. That chick of yours would have eaten him alive!"

Chancy laughed. He was proud of the chick. One day old and he had outsmarted a full-grown hawk! Chancy raised the peep to his face and admired him. He had never seen blacker, fiercer eyes on a newborn chick. It scratched and fluttered in Chancy's hands like a wild bird. Then Chancy let him walk along his arm, his bottom-heavy cottony tail

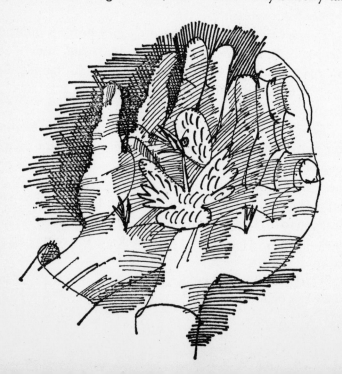

swaggering as he went. His wings shot out for balance once or twice; they were almost as small as fins on a fish, and looked foolish, but they would grow. Once at Chancy's shoulder, the chick hunkered on its frail matchstick legs and dug in with its paper-thin toenails.

Yes sir, that was a fine young rooster. Chancy thought. It had been a near calamity, but he could thank the hawk for spying out the lost bird. "That's what I'll name you!" Chancy exclaimed, strolling back with the chick sitting on his shoulder.

"Don't go naming a chicken if you expect to eat it," Uncle Will said.

"Calamity!" Chancy smiled and looked out across the river. The hawk was a mere speck over the treetops of Kentucky. "Yes sir, Uncle Will, that's his name. Calamity."

Days passed, the woodpile grew stick by stick and cord by cord, but the steamboats churned by without interest. The grub in Chancy's wheelbarrow was getting low and Uncle Will left Crow Island with a clock under his arm. He returned later in the day with a string of sausages, a whole ham and bad news.

"Chancy, there's a woodyard a couple miles upriver," he said. "They must have two, three hundred cords stacked on the bank. That's where the steamboats are wooding up. They're passing us by."

"Thunder," Chancy said. After two weeks of heavy work they were no closer to Paducah than when they had started. "Thunder and lightning."

Uncle Will laughed. "Chancy, there's more ways than one to skin a cat—or sell a load of wood." He pulled two sausages apart, tossed one to Chancy, and they sat in the shade of the barn door to eat. "We've only got to use our two heads, and anything else at hand. I've been thinking about that plunder you found washed up on the island here."

Chancy glanced over at the broken oar, the tar bucket and the arm of an old chair. They seemed almost too trifling to think about.

"How much tar is left in that bucket?" Uncle Will asked.

Chancy got up and fetched it. "Some, but not much."

"Some is enough. Set that bucket in the sun so the tar will run. Splendid! With this red slab of barn door we'll have our wood sold in no time!"

Chancy looked up in amazement.

Uncle Will cut a green willow stick about as thick as his thumb and beat one end with a rock until it was soft as a brush. Then he dipped it in the melted tar. He painted a sign that could be seen a quarter of a mile off. It read:

WOOD
$100 A CORD

Chancy gazed at it doubtfully. "Uncle Will, I do believe you priced that wood a mite expensive. Who'll buy it?"

"Nobody. But this sign will halt some steamboat captain. He'll figure that any woodseller crazy enough to price wood at a hundred dollars a cord was born for his own amusement. Wait and see. I know their breed. It shouldn't take long."

They propped the barn door against two trees, so that

the sign faced the river, and waited. All that day boats passed upriver and down, and laughter howled out across the water. But none of the boats stopped.

Early the next morning, however, a swaybacked stern-wheeler named *River Goose,* loaded with hay and passengers, gave out a guffaw with its steam whistle. The boat came strutting in alongside the island and poised itself in the current. The captain leaned out of the pilothouse window. He had a heavy round face with great muttonchop whiskers, and a watery gleam in his eye.

Uncle Will gave Chancy a sidelong glance. "Our woodpile's as good as sold," he said. "Just let me handle the talk."

Chancy nodded. Calamity liked to roost on his shoulder, and the chick sat there now watching the goings-on.

With the steamboat stopped, passengers gathered along the rails to see what was happening. The captain, peering down at the sign, shifted a cud of tobacco from one cheek to the other.

"How do, woodseller!"

"Morning, Captain," Uncle Will said. "Need any wood today?"

"Not a stick. I just wanted to see what kind of durned fool would ask a hundred dollars a cord."

"You're looking at him," Uncle Will said grandly.

The captain made a face. "What do you think you're selling? Pi-anas by the cord?"

The passengers began to snicker and smile.

"No, sir," Uncle Will answered. "If this was common firewood we'd be sellin' it at a dollar-fifty a cord. But that's not what it is. Captain, you're lookin' at an almighty rare wood. You're lookin' at twenty tight cords of pure Ohio fatwood."

"Ohio fatwood!"

"That's what I said."

The captain burst into a laugh and gave his companions in the pilothouse a wise wink. "Why, it's so rare I never heard of it!"

"I'd be surprised if you did. It don't grow anywhere but on this small island. In the old days river hogs used to come here to die. This was their burial ground."

"River hogs!"

"They're extinct now. But the roots of these trees have been feeding on hog tallow."

"They look like plain old willow to me."

"No doubt," said Uncle Will. "But it's genuine, straight-grained Ohio fatwood. Why, sir, the sap runs eighty, ninety percent pure hog fat."

"Do tell."

"Captain, this wood is so fat that one stick will drive your steamboat six to eight miles! Why, these twenty cords will power you all the way to New Orleans and partway back."

"Bunkum!" the captain howled. "You think I don't know willow when I see it?"

"I see you're a man who likes to drive a hard bargain. Captain, I'd like to sell you this fatwood. Make an offer."

"Can't use it. I just took on all I need upriver."

Uncle Will hooked a thumb in the pocket of his yellow calico vest. "Captain, I'll wager you twenty-five dollars we'll accept any offer you care to make on this entire lot of prime, straight-grain Ohio fatwood."

The captain scratched through his muttonchops. *"Any* offer?"

"That's what I said, sir. *Any offer."*

Chancy held his breath. The captain's eyes lit with glee. "You got yourself a wager, woodseller! And my passengers are witness to it."

"I see that," said Uncle Will. "What do you offer?"

"Two cents a cord."

"Sold!" said Will Buckthorn.

The entire steamboat burst into laughter. Chancy felt a hot sting of humiliation. The captain had got the best of Uncle Will. Two cents a cord! Forty cents for all their work!

In no time at all the captain called for the gangplank and directed his roustabouts to hustle the wood aboard. Uncle Will remained in the sunniest of spirits and Chancy thought his good sense had deserted him.

When the last stick of wood was aboard, the captain himself strode down the gangplank to give Uncle Will the money. "Here you are, sir," he said with expansive glee. "Forty cents. Any time you have more of that rare Ohio fatwood to sell, I'll be along."

"Thank you, Captain," said Uncle Will in a robust voice. "And now if you'll kindly pay up the twenty-five dollars."

"What's that?"

"We wagered that noble sum, sir, that I'd accept any offer you made. You offered two cents a cord. I accepted. Your very passengers are witness to it! You do owe me twenty-five dollars, Captain."

The captain's face flushed red as a sunset. The passengers

5 4

broke into a fresh round of laughter. They'd have a tale to tell. Suddenly, Chancy couldn't help laughing himself. He should have known better than to doubt Uncle Will!

The captain stood speechless for a moment, his mutton-chop whiskers trembling. But with the passengers peering down at him he had no choice but to pay off the wager. Then he stormed back up the gangplank and had it hauled in after him.

Before long he stuck his head through the pilothouse window. His mood had changed. He was chuckling. "I thought I knew every woodyard trick on the river," he said, shifting the chaw of tobacco in his cheek. "But come to think of it, that's the first time I was ever outwitted and got more'n my money's worth. That wood was worth thirty dollars. You let me have it cheap. I'm obliged to you."

He pulled in his head. Bells began to ring, the whistle cleared its throat and the stern wheel began to thrash. Soon the *River Goose* was plowing its way downriver.

Chancy looked at the twenty-five dollars. He'd never seen that much money in his entire life. "We're as good as in Paducah," he said.

Uncle Will shut one eye thoughtfully. "We can't take your flock of peeps along."

"I reckon we can sell 'em," Chancy said brightly, for now anything seemed possible with Uncle Will along. He was a grand rascal, wasn't he?

"Now let me calculate," said Uncle Will, scratching his chin. "It would be easier to sell those scrawny birds if they were big enough to eat. We can't wait for 'em to grow up."

Chancy gave a start. An idea had sprung full-blown into

his head. He was so surprised that he began to wonder if he had a touch of the grand rascal himself. "I declare, Uncle Will. There are more ways than one to skin a cat — or sell a flock of chicks."

"A splendid thought," Uncle Will nodded. "I was about to say so myself. I wonder who we can get to take that flock off our hands?"

"Shouldn't be hard," Chancy said. "There's tar left in the bucket and another side to that barn door."

6

The Log Raft

WITH THE TAR and willow stick brush Chancy set to work making a new sign. When Uncle Will read it off he roared out laughing and offered to do all the talking. That suited Chancy fine, but he made it clear that he didn't want to sell Calamity.

He sat on a stump, with Calamity roosting on his shoulder, and waited for a buyer to come along the river. The day passed. Finally crickets began tuning up for the night and gnats peppered the air. Uncle Will wound all his clocks. The flock of chicks pecked at insects.

At last there came around the upriver bend a log raft with six great sweep oars. Chancy's sign on the barn door now read:

CHICKEN DINNERS
3¢ EACH

Five raftsmen in shirtsleeves and heavy boots leaned on their oars and peered through the dusk at the sign. A bull-necked man in a brown bowler hat shouted an order. To

Chancy's delight the raft was working its way toward the island. With Uncle Will to do the talking the flock of chicks was as good as sold, he thought.

Will Buckthorn looked over the men thoughtfully. "By ginger," he said, "that raft is shorthanded. It's got six oars and five men. How would it suit you if we hitched ourselves a ride on that raft? We'd be money ahead."

Chancy had been looking forward to a steamboat ride. He looked at the raft, floating like a carpet of logs on the

river. A small shanty with a pitched roof stood in the center. There was a cookstove with a tall black chimney pipe, and laundry hanging out to dry on a sagging line. "We can see the sights as well from a raft as a steamboat, I expect. Yes, sir, Uncle Will, that would be first-rate."

Soon the raft came creaking alongside and a raftsman with hairy arms heaved a stout line ashore. Uncle Will caught it and made it fast to a stump.

The bull-necked man leaped ashore. He had short legs

and a beard like a full pitchfork of hay. He wore a faded red shirt and a wide leather belt.

"Bring on the grub!" he roared. "I'm Captain Joe Harpe, the bulliest raft pilot in sight. And the hawg-hungriest! Howdy, strangers. *Hoolah-haw!* Bring on them three-cent chicken dinners! Me and my boys'll take six each."

Will Buckthorn hooked a thumb in the pocket of his vest. "You're a mite early, Captain. Reckon you won't mind waitin' to be served."

"You reckon wrong. My mouth is a-water. Don't even bother plucking the birds — fry 'em up! We'll eat 'em feathers and all."

"Now, we'd like to oblige you, Captain — but the grub just ain't ready."

"Well, get a move on, man! How long will it take?"

"Four weeks at the soonest. And that's rushing things."

The raft pilot's great shaggy eyebrows shot aloft. "Four weeks! Stop your foolin' and rustle us up the eats. And about a bushel of corn fritters on the side."

The contest of wits was beginning. Chancy listened and watched, his gaze shifting from one speaker to the other. By dogs, it was adventuresome having Uncle Will along, he thought.

"Captain," Will Buckthorn said, shoving back his hat, "our chicken dinners have hardly got their pinfeathers yet. You can see 'em scratching around in the dirt."

Captain Harpe spied the chicks and exploded. "Confound and doggone it! Boys, it's beans and spuds for supper again tonight. Cast off!"

"Hold on," said Uncle Will. "What's wrong with eatin' your chicken dinners next month?"

"I'll be kicked by a cow! You simple-minded land-trotter, by the time you fry chicken around here, we'll be down the Mississip'."

"And still eatin' beans and spuds. Unless you'd like to

buy these chicken dinners on the hoof, so to speak, and fatten 'em up. Take 'em aboard, sir. There's plenty of room on that raft. Why, Captain, think of that mouth-watering banquet you'll have underfoot."

The raft pilot gave his bowler a hard tap. "Flap-doodle, sir! We got no time to tend poultry. Boys, let's move."

"Hold on," said Uncle Will, hooking both thumbs in his vest. "We'll sell you those chicken dinners with the feathers on — three cents each. And my young nephew standing there, Chancy B. Dundee by name, will tend them for you partway and free of charge. If he's willin'."

"I'm willin'," Chancy said quickly. His twenty-five chicks, not counting Calamity, would bring seventy-five cents — and free passage down the river.

Captain Harpe shut one eye and looked Chancy over with the other. And then his gaze returned to Uncle Will. "Stranger, what brand of kin are you to let a young'un loose on the river? He'll likely fall overboard."

"By the eternal! You're right, Captain. But we do want to oblige you. It appears to me I'd better go along to tend my nephew."

Captain Harpe's cheeks swelled up through his beard. "No, sir! We don't take *passengers*. They're worse than havin' chickens underfoot. Boys, cast off!"

"See here," said Uncle Will. "I might be persuaded to buck an oar for you — being that you're shorthanded — at least as far as Paducah. We'll want to get off there."

The raft pilot stared at Uncle Will as if he were a madman and then burst into a laugh. "Stranger — ten minutes at one of these sweeps and you'll think your back is broke in six places. Any one of my boys is strong enough to derail a train — just squintin' at it."

"They look kind of weak and sickly to me," said Uncle Will.

"Weak! Sickly!" Captain Harpe gave a huge snort and called over his shoulder. "Billy Arkansas! Come here and heft this rock."

A hulking raftsman with arms like swamp oaks stepped ashore. With a grin, he reached his large hands around a boulder near the water's edge. He heaved it to his chest with hardly a grunt, and then straight up over his head.

"Shucks," he said, setting it gently back on the ground. "This little ol' rock don't amount to a thing, Cap. Couldn't weigh more'n two hundred and fifty pounds."

Captain Harpe turned to Uncle Will. "Hear that?" he laughed. "Light as a goose feather, that rock. Let's see you raise it over *your* head, mister."

Uncle Will lit the stub of a cigar he'd been saving. Taking his time he studied the boulder. Then he bent and tried to lift it. His face went red. The rock wouldn't leave the ground. Chancy looked on with dismay. What was wrong? Any other time Uncle Will could have pitched that rock clear across the river. Why, he could pull a wagon with his teeth.

Uncle Will straightened. "Do you mind lifting it again, Mr. Arkansas? I declare, it looks impossible."

"Shucks, sir," said the raftsman. "Back home I used to load my slingshot with bigger stones than this."

And once again he lifted the heavy rock to his great chest and then up over his head.

"Hoolah-haw! How's that for weak and sickly?" Captain Harpe roared.

Uncle Will slipped Chancy a wink. Then he walked slowly around the raftsman, studying the man, puffing his cigar and taking his time. He carefully removed his slouch hat and handed it to Chancy. Then, planting his legs, he ducked his head. In the next instant Chancy was astonished to see Billy Arkansas rise in the air. Uncle Will had hoisted him on his shoulders — *stone and all!* The combined weight was so great that Uncle Will's teeth chopped his cigar in two.

"Glory be," said Captain Harpe, his little eyes snapping in awe.

"By dogs," Chancy whispered, with a rush of pride. Uncle Will could have lifted that rock all along. He had only been fooling.

"Stranger, put down that weak and sickly raftsman of mine," said Captain Harpe. "Boys, we'll tie up to this island for the night. *Hoolah-haw!* Welcome aboard, sir. You and the boy and the chickens. Stay as long as you like!"

7

The Man in the River

AT FIRST LIGHT, Captain Harpe was up and shouting. "Rise up, gents! To the oars, my lazy mud turtles! Step lively, you snoring, roaring river-rollers!"

Chancy leaped from his bedroll. He quickly gathered the chicks into the straw suitcase. Uncle Will piled their belongings in the wheelbarrow. Within moments everything was aboard the raft, and Chancy took a moment to dash the sleep from his face with river water.

Billy Arkansas cast off the lines. Uncle Will hung up his coat and vest and wrapped his two hands around a forward oar. At a shout the raftsmen began working the clumsy raft into mainstream of the river.

They were moving. Slowly Crow Island began to slip behind, and Chancy gave it a last fond look. Then he gazed at the broad river ahead. They were on their way to Paducah at last!

The air was wondrously cool and fresh. There seemed hardly a sound on the river at this hour. A bluejay sounded from the Kentucky bank, and the river picked up the dawn colors as if it were an endless winding mirror.

Chancy couldn't think of any place he'd rather be than

rafting down the Ohio on a capital fine morning like this. The log raft was drifting as lazily as a leaf with the tide; the men at the oars merely guided it on its way. They set up a slow rhythm, walking to the end of a footboard, raising the huge pine blades, returning, dipping and struggling forward again.

Chancy had never seen such gigantic oars. They stretched thirty feet long, and instead of being at the sides of the raft, where oars ought to be, they were mounted three forward and three aft. Each was balanced on a block and swiveled on a thick oak pin. The raftsmen struck him as a jolly lot, quick to laugh and with voices like bass drums. They had names like Poosh Johnson and Potato Mike and Hawg Pewitt.

Chancy tried not to get underfoot. He watered and fed the chicks. The straw suitcase was too small now to hold them and anyway they were pecking away at the straw. They'd get crop-bound. He'd have to find them larger quarters.

"Boy!"

Chancy looked up. It was Captain Harpe with his legs set three logs wide. "Yes, sir."

"Are you hungry?"

"Yes, sir."

"Can you cook?"

"No, sir."

"Ever seen it done?"

"Yes, sir."

"Well, then!" Captain Harpe exclaimed. "That qualifies you. I appoint you raft cook!"

"But, sir — "

"Nothin' fancy, you understand."

"But I don't rightly know how to cook, sir."

"How can you be sure, boy, if you ain't never tried?" The bearded pilot took a large chaw of tobacco. "We take turns aboard this raft. You just put some beans to soak for supper and some dried apples too. And boil up a pot of coffee. Make it strong, hear? Strong as tar. And fry us up a barrel of potatoes. You can't go far wrong. The first man aboard to bellyache about the grub — why, he has to do the cooking. That's the way we work it. Keeps complaints to a minimum, you know."

And off he rushed, leaving Chancy stunned. He reckoned there was nothing to do but try. He thought he knew how to boil coffee, at least.

He found a box of kindling and started a blaze in the cookstove. He filled the huge coffeepot with river water and ground up the coffee beans. That seemed like the way it was done. Soon he had the pot on the stove and regarded it as a modest achievement.

He found a huge black kettle hanging from a nail on the shanty and put a heap of beans to soak. There was a smaller pot that would do for the dried apples. Then he began peeling potatoes. He was anxious to earn his keep, but it seemed woman's work and it didn't suit his fancy. If there was a choice, he'd rather take a hand at a sweep oar. Maybe someone would complain about the grub and end his kitchen duty by the time breakfast was finished.

Once the potatoes were peeled he didn't know what to do with them. He walked forward to consult with Uncle Will.

"I'm appointed raft cook," he said.

"I declare."

"How in tarnation do you fry potatoes?"

"Did you slice 'em?"

"No, sir."

"Did you grease the pan?"

"No, sir."

"Well, then. Slice 'em. Grease the pan. Stir 'em now and then. And make the coffee strong."

Chancy returned to the cookstove. Soon the coffee was boiling away and the potatoes were sizzling. One by one, as the men were relieved at their oars, they poured a tin cup of coffee and forked themselves potatoes out of the skillet. Chancy waited for the complaints to begin.

"Best doggone coffee I ever drunk," said Billy Arkansas, helping himself to a second cup. "Sticks to the roof of your mouth — the way I like it."

"Why, as I'm alive!" said Hawg Pewitt, who walked as if he carried a water keg under each arm. "These spuds melt away on your tongue, don't they? It's like eatin' fried sunshine."

"Boy, where did you learn such fine cookin'?" asked Poosh Johnson, with a gesture of his hairy arms. "Remind me to give you my recipe for bear grease pie."

Chancy suspected he had boiled the coffee too long and that he hadn't cooked the potatoes long enough, but not even Captain Harpe protested. He bolted his breakfast and fanned his flushed face with his hat. "Bulliest grub on the river," he declared.

Chancy knew they had the best of him. He could have cooked his boots and they would have lavished praise on them. When the coffeepot was empty and the potatoes gone, he'd still be raft cook. It was a river job nobody wanted.

While the beans and dried apples soaked, Chancy emptied the kindling box and turned the chicks loose in it. It would do for a coop. He watched the men at their oars for a while, but it seemed to him the raft was hardly moving at all. Then a steamboat came rushing by and its wash sent the raft rising and dipping. Chancy was taken by surprise and knocked off his feet.

"I don't reckon you ever rode a raft before," Captain Harpe laughed.

"No, sir. Nothing this big, that is." Chancy didn't like to admit he'd never been on the river before.

"Why, boy, this raft is *small*. It's only a three-stringer. We started out with ten strings of hickory logs. Been peddling 'em off to the sawills along the river. But these last three strings are bound for New Orleans, if the river don't dry up under us before we get there — we're a mite late this year. Folks can't get enough good timber down there, the way things are building up so fast. Pay good money."

Chancy had already seen that the raft was in three long sections, butted together side by side. Each string of logs was held fast by crosswise limbs spiked down with square wooden pegs. A sweep oar was mounted at the forward and after end of each string.

"How fast do you reckon we're going?" Chancy asked.

"Mighty fast, there being no head wind," Captain Harpe answered. "A full two miles an hour, it looks like. Near takes your breath away, don't it?"

Chancy grinned. He was in no desperate hurry. Paducah would still be there when they reached it.

"Of course, the Ohio can be awful ornery," said the raft pilot. "Runs about two and a half miles to the hour, you know, but when the wind blows it almost always heads up-river. Kinda slows a raft down. First time I took a raft to New Orleans, we had head winds all the way. Took several years. When I stepped ashore I remarked how New Orleans had changed. *Hoolah-haw!* It turned out we were still in Pittsburgh, where we started from."

By early afternoon Chancy was awash in apples and beans. They were swelling and overflowing their pots. Soon he had every kettle and pan and bucket he could find heaped, and still the beans swelled and the apples overflowed. It was like tending six volcanoes at once. Finally Billy Arkansas came to his rescue with a washtub. "I do like beans and apples," he chuckled. "And you put enough to soak to last us all summer long!"

They ate beans and applesauce for supper. Beans and applesauce for breakfast. Beans and applesauce for dinner. And applesauce and beans between meals.

But not a complaint reached Chancy's ears.

When he was free of the cookstove, he attempted to teach Calamity to fan him. The chick's wings were growing out fast, with the last bits of down clinging like milkweed to the feathers.

"Fan me," Chancy would say, holding the chick on his outstretched finger. When he let his finger drop an inch or two, the chick would flutter its wings to keep its balance and give off a pleasant breeze in the heat. Before long Chancy hoped to have Calamity performing the trick on command alone.

At other times Uncle Will let Chancy give a hand at the huge sweep oar. Chancy struggled against it as if he were pushing through mud. Soon they drifted past the mouth of the Big Miami River, littered with sand bars, and Captain Harpe gave it a wide berth. Ohio was now behind them. Indiana was beginning.

They maneuvered their way, like a monstrous crab, past Rising Sun and Rabbit Hash, and still the beans and applesauce were not gone. That afternoon Chancy discovered a lump of soap missing from over the cookstove. When he ladled out supper he discovered what had happened to it.

"Doggone!" snorted Potato Mike, making a face like a dried pumpkin. "These beans taste *soapy!*"

A hush fell over the raftsmen. In an instant, Potato Mike realized his mistake. "But, boys," he grinned, straightening out his face, "if there's anything I always hungered for — it's soapy beans! Fill my plate again, Chancy lad!"

Dusk was in the air when a side-wheeler went charging past, and its wash sent the raft billowing like a carpet in a wind. Chancy set his legs to ride it out, but as he watched the steamboat he saw two figures at the stern heave something overboard.

It looked like a man.

It *was* a man. Chancy could see him thrashing about in the river. After the first shock of surprise, Chancy raised a shout. "Look! Uncle Will! Man overboard!"

Within moments Uncle Will and Billy Arkansas shoved the raft skiff into the water and went after the flailing man. The side-wheeler continued on its way without a backward glance.

It was almost dark when the skiff returned. Uncle Will carried the man over his shoulder and laid him out on the logs. "He'll be all right. But he won't need a bath for a month or so."

Chancy pressed in closer. The man was sitting up. He had lost his hat, but not his voice. "By Jacks, that was no way to treat a gentleman," he protested. "Accused me of cheating at cards, the scoundrels!"

Chancy knew that voice. He knew that red face and lumpy nose. It was Colonel Plugg.

8

The Scoundrel's Mistake

COLONEL PLUGG was soon on his legs, wet as wash, but good as new. The false eye patch was gone, but in its place was a false air of importance.

"Thank you, gentlemen, thank you," he said, clearing his throat. "I don't mind saying you caught a big fish when you hauled me out of the river. A mighty big fish. Allow me to introduce myself. Slackett's the name. *Ahem*. Senator Elwood P. Slackett, of the great and sovereign state of Illinois."

The raftsmen were duly impressed, but Chancy stood in a whirl of astonishment.

"Glory be!" exclaimed Captain Harpe, whipping off his bowler hat as if he were addressing the Stars and Stripes itself. "Welcome, sir. Billy! Fetch the senator a chair."

"We don't have any chairs, Cap."

"A keg, then! Don't keep the senator standing. Poosh! Get my blanket out of the doghouse. The senator will catch pneumony. Boy! A cup of that bully coffee of yours!"

"Tut, tut," Colonel Plugg protested. In the failing light he took no notice of Chancy. "Don't make any fuss over me, gentlemen. You've saved my life as it is, and I intend to

reward you handsomely. *Ahem.* I don't mind telling you
I'm heavily supplied with funds — "

He reached into his coat for his billfold. His jaw went
slack. Then he patted each of his wet pockets. "Gone!
Those steamboat scalawags cleaned me out! Every penny!
Confound it — after them, sir! Quick, gentlemen!"

Captain Harpe hooked the bowler back on his head.

"I'm right sorry about your billfold, Senator — but we're making top speed as it is."

The steamboat had already vanished along the meandering river. Colonel Plugg shook his fist in that direction. "Thieves! Scoundrels! Mark my word — they won't get away with this outrage! First thing in the morning I intend to take legal action. *Ahem*. Where's the coffee?"

Billy Arkansas went for the keg, Poosh Johnson hurried after the blanket, but Chancy just stood there. The mere sight of this humbug set his teeth on edge. It was clear enough that Senator Slackett, as he now chose to call himself, had been caught cheating at cards and been tossed overboard. Why, a wet ace of spades was still caught in his cuff.

Chancy could keep silent no longer. "I want my three-dollar gold piece back," he announced solemnly.

"What? What's that?"

"Colonel Plugg, I reckon you didn't expect to meet up with me again."

The impostor gave Chancy a huge squint. "Never forget a face. *Ahem*. Stand a bit closer, son, and let me look at you. What did you say your name was? Colonel Plugg? My stars! The army is taking 'em young these days! So you're Colonel Plugg, at your age. By Jacks, that beats all!"

He burst into a laugh. Oh, he was a slick one! He was twisting things around already, and Chancy's eyes glowed with rage. "I want my three dollars back," he declared.

"What's that?"

"Sir, you humbugged me out of my steamboat fare."

"Poppycock!"

Captain Harpe glowered at Chancy. "Hold your tongue, boy. That's no proper way to talk to a senator from the great and sovereign state of Illinois."

Uncle Will stepped in. "No offense, Senator. My young nephew appears to be mistaken."

Chancy's eyes flashed up in surprise. Not even Uncle Will believed him. "But it's *him*, Uncle Will! Colonel Plugg. He left me those stale eggs and ran off with my money!"

Colonel Plugg puffed up. "A monstrous charge. *Ahem*. Simply monstrous."

Uncle Will was peering at Chancy. "Didn't you tell me it was a one-eyed man who swindled you?"

"Any fool can see *I'm* a two-eyed man," laughed Colonel Plugg.

"I'll vouch for that," Captain Harpe put in. "Have a chaw of tobacco, Senator."

"No, sir," Chancy protested. "I said he was wearing an eye patch. It was a disguise — the same as his limpy leg."

"Limpy leg!" Colonel Plugg roared. "Nothing wrong with my legs — either one. By Jacks, it's a clear case of mistaken identity. *Ahem*. No harm done, lad. Now run along."

Chancy was smoldering. It was his word against the word of a senator from the great and sovereign state of Illinois. He wanted to give Colonel Plugg a smart kick to the shin. That would give him a limpy leg. "I want my gold piece, sir," he said firmly.

"Stop botherin' me, boy. Gentlemen, I'd be obliged if you'd allow me to journey down the river with you a spell.

I seem to be poverty-poor at the moment, but — *ahem* — once we reach Illinois I shall get in touch with my banker. You'll find me generous. *Ahem.* Very generous, indeed."

Uncle Will, taking it all in, gave Chancy a sharp nod. Chancy saw that he was beaten. He clamped his jaws and wandered away. Uncle Will joined him at the rear of the shanty and began chuckling. "Chancy," he said. "You hung on like a bulldog."

"It's him, Uncle Will! It's Colonel Plugg, sure as sunrise."

"No doubt."

Chancy gazed up. "You believe me?"

"Of course I do. Why, that man is so sharp and crooked you could use him for a corkscrew. It was all I could do to keep from throwing him back in the river."

"It was?" Chancy's spirits brightened like a fanned ember.

"But that wouldn't get your gold piece back, would it?" Uncle Will scratched through his curly hair. "On the other hand, he could be telling the truth. He's got empty pockets, no doubt, and you can't draw cider from an empty jug."

"Reckon not," Chancy said.

"And you can't rub human nature the wrong way, either. I'm talking about Captain Harpe."

"He just won't listen to the truth."

"Oh, he's listening, Chancy, but he don't want to hear it. Why, he's proud as a peacock to have a genuine senator aboard. He's not of a mind to let you cheat him out of the pleasure. That's the human nature of it. Patience is the answer. Patience is my advice. He'll come to his senses. Just let Colonel Plugg blow himself full of his own wind. He's bound to make some mistake, and then we'll let the air out of him. Won't that be something to see! I'm not sayin' you'll ever see that gold piece again, but the laugh alone ought to be worth three dollars!"

They tied up that night along the Kentucky side of the river. Poosh Johnson hung red and green lanterns to the corners of the raft to warn off steamboats.

Chancy kept his distance from Colonel Plugg. He wasn't sure he cared about his lost gold piece anymore. They had their woodyard money. But he wanted to see Colonel Plugg get his comeuppance. He began to polish his buckeye hopefully.

The raftsmen were soon telling stories and slapping at mosquitoes. Billy Arkansas cleaned his long-barreled squirrel gun. Uncle Will wound his clocks. And Colonel Plugg sat like a Roman emperor on a molasses keg and chewed Captain Harpe's finest tobacco. While his clothes were hanging out to dry, he wore Captain Harpe's Sunday suit. And he slept that night wrapped in Captain Harpe's army blanket.

All night long mosquitoes whined in the air. Rolled up on the hard logs, Captain Harpe flailed his neck and forehead from one hour to the next. Chancy felt sorry for him, growling and grumbling and groaning while Colonel Plugg snored contentedly from the cocoon he had made of the blanket.

Chancy was not surprised to see Captain Harpe some-

what out of sorts the next day. The raft pilot had hardly
got a wink of sleep. And he fared little better the following
night.

Chancy went about his chores at the cookstove and
Uncle Will said, "The human nature of it is beginning to
turn in our favor. Make the coffee a mite stronger."

That suppertime Chancy made the coffee so strong it
would hardly pour. Colonel Plugg took a mouthful and he
was a full minute trying to spit it out. "Where in tarnation
did that Ohio farm boy learn to make coffee? This infernal
stuff sticks to the roof of the mouth!"

A stunned silence settled over the raftsmen. Smiles were
barely hidden. By dogs, now the rascal has put his foot in,
Chancy thought. He'll be peeling potatoes for breakfast.

But Captain Harpe, with great sagging eyes, peered at his guest. "Senator," he said slowly. "We don't complain about the grub on this raft. I reckon it ain't fit and proper for a senator from the great and sovereign state of Illinois to serve at the cookstove, so we'll overlook what you said. I'm turning in. I ain't been sleeping much lately."

Chancy wanted to protest — fair was fair — but he saw that it was useless. Uncle Will gave him a long glance. Patience, he seemed to say. A mite more patience.

Chancy's patience ran out just before dawn. He awoke with a great start. A revelation had come over him like a thundergust. He could *prove* that Senator Slackett was the same Colonel Plugg he had met before on the road!

He wanted to wake Uncle Will. Then he decided not to. He guessed he ought to do his own talking. For a moment he listened to Colonel Plugg snoring like a bullfrog. Not far off Captain Harpe was still trying to find a soft place on the hickory logs and fending off mosquitoes. Chancy guessed that *his* patience had run out too.

Chancy left his blanket and crossed the logs. "You awake, Captain Harpe?" he whispered.

"What? What?"

Chancy cleared his throat. "Well, sir, like Uncle Will said all along — that varmint was bound to trip over his own tongue, sooner or later."

"Varmint? Varmint?"

"That impostor snoring away in your blanket. The truth is he's no more a senator than I am, sir — he as well as admitted it at suppertime. He's the man who made off with my gold piece back in Ohio."

Captain Harpe was thoroughly weary of the hard logs

and fully awake now. He gave his neck a resounding slap that missed the mosquito but woke the chicks. "Admitted it, you say?"

"Yes, sir. There hasn't been a mortal word spoken on this raft about where I'm from. You raftsmen don't ask questions."

"That's true. We don't."

"But when he choked on his coffee — he called me an Ohio farm boy. Uncle Will knows it, and I know it — but how did *he* know it? Because that's where we met, back on that farm road in Ohio when he tricked me out of my money — exactly the way I tried to tell you."

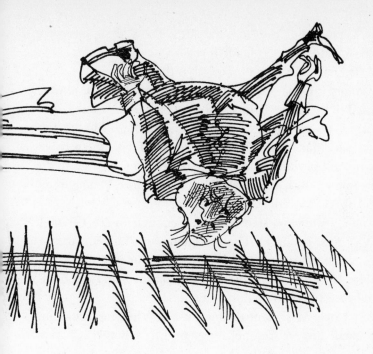

Captain Harpe was silent for a moment and then leaped
to his feet. *"Hoolah-haw!"*

He lurched to the snoring figure of Colonel Plugg, got
hold of the blanket and whipped it free. The swindler
went spinning over several logs. It woke him up, and the
other raftsmen as well.

Captain Harpe roared at him like a bear. "Rise up, you
tallow-nosed windbag!"

Colonel Plugg's face swelled with outrage. "What! What!
This is monstrous, sir!"

"I declare," said Captain Harpe, "if you don't look like
the hind end of bad luck. I do hate to disturb your slum·

ber, Senator, but the boys will be wantin' their morning coffee — and you ain't made it yet."

"*Me*, sir! What kind of waggery is this?"

Captain Harpe raised such an angry scowl it almost glowed in the dark. "Did you think you had me fooled, you infernal, wormy-eyed, chin-flapping humbug? There's the cookstove. Make the coffee strong as tar! That's the way we like it. And peel up a barrel of potatoes. You're going to do the cooking aboard this raft. Hop to it before I change my mind and wrap a hickory log around your neck!"

Chancy was now standing close enough to see Colonel Plugg's face go slack. The raftsmen were ranged around him and he clearly saw that further argument would be useless. He slunk away toward the cookstove, and the raftsmen broke into a three-dollar laugh.

But Uncle Will slept through it all. When he awoke he was startled to see Colonel Plugg peeling potatoes. Chancy was dangling his feet in the river and polishing his buckeye.

9

Chancy's Axe

THE FLOCK of chicks was outgrowing the kindling box. They scratched and fluttered over the logs and Chancy tended them like a shepherd. He fed them corn grits out of his hand and dug worms on the banks at night. Calamity rode his shoulder like a young falcon.

From dawn to dusk Uncle Will and the raftsmen strode against the sweep oars. Colonel Plugg sat filling tub after tub with peeled potatoes and mumbling to himself like a fallen emperor. Chancy wasted hardly a thought on him. Louisville and the Falls of the Ohio were approaching and he became aware of an air of expectancy aboard the raft.

The skiff, the stove and the raft tools were lashed down. Billy Arkansas checked the tie logs to make sure the raft would hold together. Captain Harpe kept squinting at the river and shaking his head.

"Only a blessed fool would run the Falls this time of year," he declared. "Gents, reckon I'm a fool. If the river drops any lower we'll be raising dust with our oars. But we're takin' the Falls. Never mind Louisville. We ain't stoppin'. I tell you we'll wish we had another foot of water when we hit the chute. We'll be lucky if we don't pile up like matchsticks." He gave a snort and a laugh. "Now rest easy, boys. You'll be busier'n a fiddler's elbow in another couple hours."

Chancy was keen to go adventuring down the Ohio, but he wondered if it might be a better idea to walk the rest of the way to Paducah. Plunging over a waterfall on three strings of hickory logs didn't strike him as altogether judicious. He shot Uncle Will a glance, but Uncle Will continued whistling pleasantly at his work. The raft drifted along with the current, the six long oars twitching like cat's whiskers.

The river widened and Louisville rose out of the bear grass at a bend on the Kentucky bank. There were so many buildings that Chancy couldn't begin to count them. He could see horses and buggies everywhere along the streets. At the landing, great white steamboats clustered like suckling pigs. Chancy longed to go ashore and see the great sights, but Captain Harpe hardly gave the city a second glance. The Falls of the Ohio lay ahead.

A river ferry bore down on them, its whistle screaming. Captain Harpe ignored it. Before long Chancy could see white water ahead. He herded the flock of chicks into the kindling box and lashed his blanket over the top. The knotholes would let in air. Then he found a safe place for his axe and tied down the wheelbarrow.

"Hard over, boys!" shouted Captain Harpe. "There's deeper water on the Indiana side!"

Moments later the raft went bucking and heaving over broken water. Spray shot into the summer day and lit up like swarms of fireflies. Chancy stretched himself along a tie log and held on like a barnacle. The raft shuddered and stretched and groaned. The men bent their backs against the long sweeps, steering as best they could through the rapids.

Chancy's teeth were almost jarred loose. He clenched his jaws and turned his head. He could see the chicks bouncing away under the blanket. But the thought of the falls ahead took his breath away. Suddenly the raft went slipping down a long chute where the water raced in shallow glassy sheets over broad limestone shelves.

The oarsmen stayed on their feet, fighting the swift current and clinging with their curled toes. They were already wet as watersnakes. At every moment Chancy expected to see Uncle Will flung into the air. Captain Harpe worked his arms like pump handles and shouted above the roar of water. The chute seemed miles long to Chancy and they hadn't even arrived at the Falls yet.

From moment to moment the logs scraped rock. "Spit, boys, spit!" Captain Harpe barked. "We need all the water we can get!"

Suddenly Uncle Will and the forward logs dove out of sight. Chancy hardly had time to gasp. The rest of the raft went plunging after them, as if they had slid off the edge of the earth. But it was only a shallow dam, and the logs leveled out in smooth water.

Still Chancy held on. His knuckles were white as bone. The side of his face was scraped raw. This could only be the calm before the storm, and he waited.

But soon Captain Harpe was towering over him. "Asleep, boy?"

"No, sir!" Chancy said. "How much further to those infernal falls?"

Captain Harpe's eyes popped. *"Hoolah-haw!* Wasn't that ride woolly enough to suit you? You just came over the Falls, sonny — three miles of 'em."

Chancy lifted his head and looked back. He sat up. If he'd known *that* was the Falls of the Ohio he would have enjoyed it twice as much.

Captain Harpe burst into a laugh. "You want to turn back and ride 'em again?"

Chancy brushed himself off. "I don't mind, sir," he said. "If it wouldn't be too much trouble."

It was the laziest time of Chancy's life. Outside of tending the chicks, he occupied himself watching the river unwind. Day by day the bluffs gave way to woodlands and flats. The horizon stretched further and further away. Endless flights of passenger pigeons crossed the river in fluttering blue streamers. Hour after hour the summer sun beat down, and occasionally a thundershower would arrive like an act of mercy.

Each small river town was an event and he'd gaze at the cobbled landings and boat stores and charging ferries. He might grow up to be a coming-and-going man like Uncle

Will, free as the wind, with no end of things to do and new sights to see.

But at night Uncle Will talked more and more of giving up his ways and finding a place to roost. "A family like us — once we round up Indiana and Mirandy and little Jamie — why, we can't be coming-and-going all the while. It's time I made somethin' of myself. I'd like you young'uns to be proud of me."

"I'm proud of you as you stand, Uncle Will," Chancy said earnestly.

"By the eternal — there's no telling where a man like me could end up. Governor, even! I tell you, Chancy, I feel a stirrin' of ambition. I hear it singing in my ears like meadowlarks on a spring morning. A family man ought to amount to something."

Then Uncle Will wound his clocks and went to sleep.

Well, they were a long way from settling down, Chancy told himself. They hadn't as much as found Indiana yet, and he might be grown before they turned up Mirandy and little Jamie.

In the days that followed Chancy was hard put to find enough feed for the chicks. They wanted to eat all the time and had grown as fat as pigeons. He dipped a stick in molasses and caught waterbugs and grasshoppers and other insects on the wing. He let them peck for grit in the dirt early in the morning, and eat fresh grass off the banks. They needed full crops to digest their food and he assured himself their crops were forming by feeling for hard lumps low on their necks. Their combs were growing out yellow as corn between their eyes.

In the hottest part of the day he'd sit in the shade of the

doghouse and let Calamity peck at his shirt buttons or at his teeth. He'd say "Fan me" and sometimes Calamity would. Then Chancy would offer a grasshopper or a water-bug as reward. It was astonishing what a fine breeze Calamity's rusty-red wings could beat up.

"I'll be surprised if we're not in Paducah by Thursday," Captain Harpe said. Three days! Chancy almost began to count the hours. They tied up that night along a Kentucky canebrake, and awoke the next morning to find that Colonel Plugg had departed in the night.

"That man was harder to get rid of than a wart," Captain Harpe laughed. "Boys, cast off."

The oarsmen went to their sweeps and the raft worked its way into the current. But within a minute or two Billy Arkansas discovered that his squirrel gun was missing. Captain Harpe found that his Sunday suit had disappeared — with his money pouch in a pocket. And with horror Chancy saw that his four-pound axe was gone.

A bolt of lightning couldn't have stunned him more. He stared at the wheelbarrow. It couldn't be true! But it was. His Pa's axe was missing.

Uncle Will bristled. "That ornery, low-down blackleg! He must have teethed on brimstone!"

"I'll snatch him baldheaded!" Captain Harpe declared, pulling his hat furiously down over his ears. "I'll skin him with my living hands!"

Billy Arkansas was so hopping mad he looked set to leap the river and start tearing up the cane patch. "Head 'er in, Cap! I'm goin' ashore!"

Captain Harpe ordered the raft back to the bank, and for an hour the raftsmen went crashing through the sorghum. They didn't turn up so much as a footprint. Finally Captain Harpe called them back to the raft. He was breathing live steam. "Boys, that skunk is long gone. If we go flea-jumping around the countryside we'll get stuck in the dust all summer with three strings of logs. Look at that river! It's already lower than a snake's belly. It pains me to say it, boys, but we've got to move while there's still moisture under us."

Chancy's eyes flashed to Uncle Will. "I aim to stay," he

declared flatly. "Uncle Will, I intend to get my Pa's axe back."

"We'll stay, the both of us," Uncle Will nodded. And he turned to the raft pilot. "If we can't out-run that double-jawed, chicken-livered, tallow-faced varmint — by the eternal, we'll out-calculate him!"

Captain Harpe bit off a large chaw of tobacco and handed it around. "He's took to the woods like a bear to a honey-tree, and he'll stay hid. That's why he took along Billy's squirrel gun and Chancy's axe."

"That's what he wanted us to believe — but that's not the way I calculate it," said Uncle Will, his cat's eyes set at a keen squint. "A humbug like Colonel Plugg won't head for the woods — not if there was cash money in your pouch."

"More'n sixty dollars — the thieving, low-hound reprobate. Why, if he ever crosses my path again I'll give him such a high kick he won't come down for several generations!"

"I know exactly where we'll find him," said Will Buckthorn.

Captain Harpe lifted the hat off his ears. "*Exactly*, did you say?"

"*Precisely*," said Uncle Will. "A man like Colonel Plugg, always putting on airs — just calculate the human nature of it. With sixty-odd dollars in the pocket of your Sunday suit — why, he'll make for the *best* hotel and buy himself the *best* room and *that's* where we'll find him."

The darkness lifted from Captain Harpe's face. "*Hoolah-haw!*" he laughed. And then the shadows returned. "But confound and doggone it! Which way did he go?"

"Either upriver or down," said Uncle Will, the soul of confidence, as usual. "You're floating downriver — just have a look in the towns along the way. Chancy and I will march upriver as far back as Shawneetown and Uniontown. He can't have got any further than that. If you don't find him — most likely asleep in some hotel — by ginger, we will."

"Boys," said Captain Harpe. "What are we standing here for?"

The crew leaped along the logs to the sweep oars. Chancy and Uncle Will left their belongings aboard, so as to travel light, but Chancy snatched up Calamity. That bird would be forlorn without him.

He stood with Uncle Will in the canebrake and watched the raft drift away.

"We'll meet you in Paducah!" Uncle Will shouted.

10

The Ostrich and the Snapping Turtle

CHANCY pulled his straw hat resolutely over his eyes and picked up a stone. It wouldn't surprise him if Colonel Plugg jumped out of the canebrake at them. That man was infernally cunning.

Uncle Will led the way along a narrow road and Chancy kept his eyes peeled. Before long they came to a ramshackle molasses mill abuzz with flies. There was no sign of Colonel Plugg or anyone else. The sorghum was not yet ripe enough to harvest.

Yet here and there a stalk was turning yellow, with seed clusters rising at the top. Chancy fed seeds to Calamity, and he and Uncle Will chewed out the cane juice while tramping further upriver. It was all the breakfast they could find.

"He might have pitched the squirrel gun in the river," Chancy said dismally. "My axe, too."

"Oh, he's ornery enough," Uncle Will nodded. "But they are worth cash money. He has in mind to sell them."

They walked a little further and Chancy said, "It's not likely he met anyone in the dark who would buy that plunder."

"Not likely at all."

Chancy felt reassured. It was still early morning and if they hurried they might catch the rascal asleep, as Uncle Will had said.

They hardly met a soul along the river. But when they did, they stopped briefly to describe Colonel Plugg and the squirrel gun and the axe with the fine black cherry handle. If the scoundrel had come this way he hadn't been observed.

Uncle Will lengthened his stride and Chancy had to step lively to keep up. At noon they stood looking at Shawneetown across the river. Chancy could see three or four hotels and he almost fancied he could hear Colonel Plugg snoring in one of them.

They had to wait for the ferry. But once on the Illinois side of the river they made a beeline for the best hotel. Then they tried the second best and the third best and on to the worst, until there were no hotels left in town to search. It was clear that Colonel Plugg was not to be found in Shawneetown.

Pausing only long enough to bolt a meal of fried catfish, Chancy and Uncle Will continued upriver. It was a hot, dusty march and Chancy would be glad to see the sun go down. Calamity rode his shoulder in the shade of his straw hat.

They reached Uniontown late in the night. No man answering Colonel Plugg's description had been seen and Chancy's hopes faded.

But Uncle Will remained the soul of optimism. "By ginger," he laughed. "It looks like we got him captured."

"Captured?" said Chancy.

"That humbug went *down*river. That's plain now. It

wouldn't surprise me if Captain Harpe and the boys have already pounced on him!"

Chancy touched the lump the buckeye made in his hip pocket. He had been disgusted with it all day. It seemed to him the most temperamental buckeye ever grown. If it was supposed to bring good luck, how had Colonel Plugg managed to make off with his Pa's axe? But finally Chancy dug out the buckeye and began to polish it. He'd give it another chance.

"I don't see any reason why we shouldn't have ourselves a steamboat ride," said Uncle Will. "Unless you'd rather walk to Paducah."

"No, sir," said Chancy. "I'd *like* a steamboat ride."

Torches lit up the steamboat landing. Yellow flames fluttered from black iron baskets hung on poles; the night air was scented with burning pine chips and resin. They looked over an ancient side-wheeler due to leave in the morning with a deck cargo of onions. Her narrow decks were warped, her paint was peeling and her woodwork was pocked with bullet holes. She was the *Snapping Turtle*. They learned from the roustabouts that she had been shot up during the war, sunk, refloated, and had more lives than a cat.

"How does she take your eye?" Uncle Will asked.

"By dogs! I never saw a steamboat that I liked better," Chancy answered. That was a monstrous exaggeration, but the *Snapping Turtle* would get them to Paducah the following afternoon, and Chancy didn't intend to be particular.

"Let's hunt up the mud clerk and get ourselves a cabin," Uncle Will said.

They found the purser, a long-haired riverman, with his feet propped on his desk.

"A cabin for two," said Uncle Will.

Over the tops of his sweaty glasses the purser looked doubtfully at the bird perched on Chancy's shoulder. "Excuse me, gents," he said. "But do you mean to bring that chicken along?"

"We don't mean to leave it behind," said Uncle Will.

"Well, sir, then you'll have to go deck passage. We don't allow chickens in the cabins."

Uncle Will shoved back his hat. "Of course you don't, but that bird ain't a chicken," he said. "You're not the first to make that mistake, no sir. So we'll be obliged if you would point out our cabin."

The purser's glasses slid lower on his nose. "If that ain't a chicken what do you call it, sir?"

Uncle Will shook his head. "I was hoping you wouldn't ask that. I'm not anxious for word to get around. Folks would pester us half to death."

"I won't tell a soul," said the mud clerk.

Uncle Will hesitated. Then he bent closer and lowered his voice. He was straight-faced as a deacon. "I don't expect you to believe this, sir — but that bird happens to be an ostrich. Full grown, too."

The purser's jowls sagged. Chancy's eyebrows lifted. The thought took his breath away. It was a wonder to him how Uncle Will could stretch a young chicken into a full-grown ostrich. It was a wonder to the purser as well, but he was quick to recover from the surprise. He licked his lips and rose to the occasion with a relish. The duel of wits was on.

"Ain't that bird kind of *small* for an ostrich?" he said.

"No, sir," Uncle Will replied. "It's not generally known, but ostriches never get any bigger than that. I was as surprised as you are to learn that."

"Glory," said the purser. "You expect me to swallow that, sir?"

"I was hoping you would," Uncle Will grinned. "But I may have been departin' slightly from the facts. I'll admit that. The bona fide, rock-bottom, guaranteed facts are so hard to believe that you'd think I was trying to string up a bunch of nonsense."

"Not for a moment," protested the purser. "I can see you're a man who pays close attention to the truth, and I don't intend to settle for anything else."

Chancy never saw two more sober faces. It was as if the merest glimmer of a smile would break the rules and ruin the contest, with the cabin at stake.

"Well, sir," said Uncle Will, "there's a thing or two you'll have to know about ostriches. Where they come from it don't rain more'n once every couple of hundred years. They can't take water. When an ostrich keels over in the heat you don't want to throw a bucket of water to revive the poor devil. You throw dust. That's what they're used to. But we didn't know that and last summer in Kansas — it was just north of Wichita — that bird you're looking at keeled over in the sun. We did the same thing I reckon you'd have done."

"Threw a bucket of water at it?"

"Exactly."

"And what happened?"

"Why, sir — that ostrich shrunk."

The purser's jaw dropped. "Glory," he breathed.

"I wouldn't believe it myself," said Uncle Will, straightening, "if I hadn't seen it with my own eyes."

The purser tapped his fingertips together thoughtfully. "I do hate to tell you this," he said, "but your ostrich shrunk into a barnyard chicken, and we don't allow chickens in the cabins."

Uncle Will was not beaten.

"Does the steamboat have any rules against an ostrich?" he asked.

"None at all."

"Have you ever seen a bona fide, rock-bottom, guaranteed ostrich before?"

"Never."

"In that case," said Uncle Will, "how can you be *sure* you're not looking at one right now?"

The purser pulled at his ear and squinted at Chancy and Calamity. Finally he gave a nod. "By gum, sir, you've got a point. That's true. I've been leaning on hearsay evidence, but facts is facts. Why, I'm ashamed of myself. *That's an ostrich.* I can see it now. Definite resemblance. I'll put the three of you in cabin seven. The boy there goes half price. I'll have to charge for the ostrich, though. And since it's *full*-grown, as you said — why, sir, I'll have to charge you *full* fare."

With hardly a pause Uncle Will hooked his thumbs in his calico vest and turned to Chancy.

"Nephew, it's everlasting *expensive* to travel with an ostrich. Full fare. Imagine that. I didn't reckon on it. By the eternal, we'd be money ahead to let folks believe that bird is just a barnyard chick — and travel deck passage with the onions."

Uncle Will was still chuckling in the morning when the *Snapping Turtle* gave a blast of her whistle and began kicking up spray. He didn't mind losing the battle of nonsense with the mud clerk — he hadn't expected to win it. "Let it be a lesson to you, Chancy."

"Not to tell lies?"

"Bless me, no," said Uncle Will, brushing flakes of onion skin off his coat. "A whopper never hurt anyone, if it's tall enough. It's pleasurin' I'm talking about. You got to make your own at times. If you know you're going to sleep on onions anyway — why, you might as well sleep with a smile as a frown."

Belching black smoke, the steamboat carried them down the river. It coughed and wheezed and shook. Chancy could hardly restrain his excitement. They were on their way to Paducah at last!

He spent a good part of the morning exploring the boat. He stood at the open door of the engine room, breathing the smell of warm oil and watching the massive machinery at work. With bursts of steam a huge piston slid back and forth like a battering ram. Cranks turned, rods rose and fell, and valves opened and shut. Everywhere, brass and steel shone like gold and silver. The wonders in the room held Chancy fascinated. He had never before seen anything more complicated than a water pump. This was a marvel. The only familiar thing was the spittoon at the engineer's feet.

Before long he had worked his way to the top deck and gazed at the glass box where the captain was spinning the wheel. The steamboat was stepping along at a lively pace, wriggling like a fish through the shallow channel. At the rate they were moving, Chancy thought, they ought to be catching up with the drifting raft in a matter of hours.

The upper deck was hot as a skillet and Chancy soon dove for the shade of the cargo deck. He let Calamity have some water out of the dipper and finally settled himself with Uncle Will on the sacks of onions.

"Seen everything?" said Uncle Will.

"Most everything." Chancy's eye lit on a bullet hole in the woodwork. "You reckon the lead's still in there?"

"It wouldn't surprise me."

"Would they mind if I dug it out?"

"You'd be doing them a favor," said Uncle Will, handing Chancy his Barlow knife. "How much do you recall about the folks who took your sister to Paducah?"

Chancy set to work. "They were named Jones, I remember that."

Uncle Will pursed his lips. "They shouldn't be hard to find with an odd, unusual name like that. Jones. Do you recollect if Mr. Jones had a first name?"

"No, sir. He was a chair bottomer, just passing through. I only saw him once, and that was at night. He had a turkey neck."

Uncle Will said no more, and Chancy kept burrowing with the knife. He could hardly wait to see Indiana's face when they surprised her. Any other girl might faint dead away — but not Indiana, he thought. She was too contrary to do a thing like that. By dogs, she might not even be glad to see him. Even after four years she might not have forgiven him for letting that Kentucky-bound chair bottomer take her away. But hadn't he tried? Hadn't he run away six times trying to follow the wagon, even after it was long gone?

Of course, Indiana was grown up some now, and he told himself she'd be overjoyed at the sight of him. He wondered if she still had the corn husk doll Mama had made for her. As he recollected, it was named Tollie, and he remembered how she had clung to it sitting up on the wagon the night she had gone.

Like a pulled tooth the bullet came squeaking out of the wood. It was a misshapen lump of lead, but Chancy admired it enormously. He held it to the light like a jewel and then bounced it in his hand, taking the heft of it. Just imagine, he thought, this bullet was shot in the war. He meant to keep it and slipped it into his hip pocket with the buckeye.

Just before noon Captain Harpe's raft loomed ahead as a dark splotch on the river. Chancy and Uncle Will jumped to their feet. The whistle began to scream as if to blast the raft of hickory logs out of its path, but Captain Harpe wasn't giving up an inch of water.

Chancy climbed on the bull rail, and he and Uncle Will yelled and waved their arms.

"Captain Harpe!"

"Billy Arkansas! We're here!"

But their voices were drowned out by the thumping and splashing of the paddlewheels and the roar of the whistle. The steamboat edged by, passing up the raft as if it were standing still.

Quickly, Chancy tried to spy out his axe. He could see chicks everywhere — but no axe. And then the raft slipped behind them, rolling in great billows over the wake. Captain Harpe finally looked up to shake his fist at the steamboat.

Chancy glanced at Uncle Will. He couldn't entirely hide his disappointment. But Uncle Will was undaunted. "Why, that axe was there in the doghouse waiting for you," he said. "Sure as sunrise."

Chancy took a breath. "I wouldn't be a bit surprised," he said, having something to hang his hopes on.

Later, with long shouts of its steam whistle, the *Snapping Turtle* came charging around a last bend. And there was the mouth of the Tennessee. And there was a town, sprawling in the heat and dust of the flat Kentucky bank. Chancy stood on the rail and watched. He didn't have to be told. He knew. He was looking at Paducah.

11

The Chair Bottomer

PADUCAH! Chancy tried to look everywhere at once. He had dreamed of this moment and now Paducah stretched before his eyes like a fabled place. Buildings shouldered one another up and down the long streets. Tall brick chimneys rose like spires from the sawmills and tanneries and poured smoke into the summer sky. Low wooded hills reached back to the horizon.

Chancy tried not to let his excitement show. Along the river front a sloping wharf stood at the foot of town like a broad front porch. Horses and mules, drays and wagons clattered across the planks. Shouts filled the air as roustabouts struggled with great barrels of tobacco and bales of cotton.

The engine-room bells jingled festively in Chancy's ears. Whistle blaring, the steamboat bullied its way through the tugs and wharf boats to the landing.

A small crowd was waiting for the gangplank to be run out and Chancy half expected to catch sight of his sister Indiana. She wouldn't be there — he knew that — but he couldn't help peering at the faces. He looked for two flying

pigtails; that was the way he remembered her. He'd know her right off — he was sure of it.

Uncle Will turned to him with a broad smile. "Shall we step ashore and hunt up that chair bottomer?"

"We likely could find Indiana before supper," Chancy said.

"Might."

Chancy lifted Calamity to his shoulder and they strode across the gangplank. As they picked their way through the crowd, past the Southern Hotel and along the dusty streets, Chancy seemed to see pigtails flying everywhere. They walked along the street until they came to a furniture store.

"Howdy, sir," said Uncle Will to the proprietor. "Can you tell us where we might find a chair bottomer named Jones?"

The proprietor was a heavy gentleman with a palm leaf fan in his hand. "Jones, suh?" he said, cooling his face with the fan. "You mean Micajah Jones — that low-down craw-fish who makes hickory chairs over on the Tennessee?"

"Most likely," said Uncle Will.

"A gander-necked man with a nose like a stick?"

"That's him," said Chancy.

"Why, yes indeedy, I can direct you to him, stranger. There's not a soul in Paducah who don't know that cussed old skinflint. If he ain't the meanest man in town I'll be surprised. It wouldn't be fair not to warn you, suh."

Uncle Will rubbed his jaw thoughtfully. "Mean as that, is he?"

"Mean as his hide will hold," said the furniture man, briskly fanning his face. "Why, suh, that man feeds his dogs better'n his wife and young'uns — and his dogs is half-starved."

"That's mean," Uncle Will admitted, exchanging a glance with Chancy.

"Miserly, too. Why, suh, old Micajah won't hardly sit down for fear he'll wear out the seat of his britches."

"That's miserly," said Uncle Will.

"And them's just his *best* points," the proprietor added. "If you got a dollar in your pocket, hold onto it with both hands. If he gets the scent of money he'll trick you out of it, suh. He could bamboozle a skunk out of the stripe on its back. I declare, if anyone ever got the best of him — old Micajah would bite himself."

Soon Chancy and Uncle Will were on their way again, their heads full of directions. When they reached the Tennessee River at the edge of town they were to follow the bank for a mile. They'd find a two-story frame house on stump ground and know it for sure by a tall persimmon tree on the west side of the house.

Along the riverbank, Chancy spied a broken strongbox moldering in the leaves. He was for making use of it. "We could bury our woodyard money, Uncle Will."

"It's safe enough in my coat pocket. Mr. Jones won't

sniggle us out of it. Why, he'll find it easier to eat a wasp's nest — with the wasps still in it."

It was mid-afternoon when they saw the tall persimmon tree and the house slouching in its shadow. Chancy didn't like the look of the place. With old tree stumps standing all about, the house seemed set among tombstones. There was no one stirring except for three gaunt dogs, who began to bark. Sight unseen, Micajah Jones filled Chancy with dread. But behind the sagging front door Chancy expected to find his sister Indiana, and the thought made his scalp prickle.

The dogs came bounding toward them. They were so thin that Chancy fancied he could hear their bones rattling as they ran. They barked and growled and paused to scratch fleas. In no time at all Uncle Will was making friends with them. Then a man stepped out of a sway-backed shed in the rear with a shotgun across his arms.

"You there! Stop annoyin' my hounds!"

Chancy recognized the man at once — the sharp-nosed, long-necked man who had taken Indiana away four years before.

"We're not annoying your dogs," said Uncle Will. "They look almighty hungry."

"Clear off, stranger, unless you want to dodge buckshot."

"We came looking for Mr. Micajah Jones, the chair bottomer."

The man shut one eye. "What you want of him?"

Uncle Will walked forward, with Chancy and the dogs following close behind. "It wouldn't surprise me if you're the man we're looking for."

"Maybe I am and maybe I ain't."

"We came a long way to find you, sir," said Uncle Will. Chancy was quite content to let him do the talking. "Any objection if we sit down and talk?"

"We can stand up and talk," said the chair bottomer, holding onto the shotgun. He regarded the two strangers with guarded, deep-set eyes. His face was narrow and bony, and almost as red as brick. He wore a large black hat with no shape to it at all, and his wrists hung out below his sleeves. If he recognized Chancy he gave no sign of it.

"You won't be needing that gun," said Uncle Will.

"Might and might not. Reckon you didn't come a long way to buy a hickory chair."

"That's true," said Uncle Will. "And I can see you're a man who gets directly to the point. Well, sir, the point is this. You were traveling through Erie County, Ohio, some years ago and were kindly enough to take in an orphan girl."

"Maybe I did and maybe I didn't."

Uncle Will shoved back his hat. "I'm talking about Indiana Dundee, sir, and no maybes about it."

Micajah Jones lowered his wispy eyebrows. "Keep a-talkin'."

"Allow me to introduce my young companion. This is Chancy Dundee — Indiana's older brother."

The chair maker's mouth gave a twitch of surprise. Then he cleared his throat and rubbed his chin. "Bless me — all the way from Erie County. Why, I almost didn't recognize you, boy."

Chancy took a breath. "I wonder could I see my sister now, sir?"

"Come in out of the sun, the both of you. I'd invite you to supper, but we already had ours."

They followed Micajah Jones into the shed and Uncle Will slipped Chancy a sly smile. It was far short of supper-time. The chair bottomer didn't intend to put himself out for them, and that suited Chancy fine. All he wanted was to get hold of Indiana and run.

Inside the shed, new hickory chairs hung from the rafters and wood chips were as thick as leaves on the floor. The air was heavy with the odor of hot glue. Toward the back Chancy saw a chair half bottomed with cane. Pegs were stuck in the rail holes and split cane coiled like loose wire on the floor. He lifted Calamity from his shoulder and let the chick forage among the wood chips.

"Chancy Dundee," said Micajah Jones, clucking his tongue. He gave a dry laugh, like sandpaper being rubbed together. "Why, I remember I almost chose to take you instead of that sister of yours."

"I didn't know that," Chancy murmured.

"I'd have learned you to cane a good chair. But boys is always running away. Girls is easier to keep a leash on — except little Indiana. I made a mistake offerin' to take her along home with me. If I wasn't a kindly man I'd have long ago sold her to gypsies."

A flush of anger rose to Chancy's face. "Might I see her, sir?" he asked.

"Fed and clothed that girl and she acts like she was doing *me* a favor. Never saw such a high-headed child. I've had to whip her many a time, but there's not a tear in that young'un."

Uncle Will was studying the man with a cold eye. "You have our sympathy," he said.

"You come to visit, I expect," said the chair bottomer.

"No, sir," answered Uncle Will. "We came to fetch her."

Micajah Jones hardly blinked an eye. He began scratching his chin. "Well, now, that's too bad. It looks like you come a long way for nothing."

"It don't look that way to me," said Uncle Will. "From what you've said, sir, she's little use to you."

"That's true. The girl ain't been worth her keep."

"Then you'll be glad to shout for her, and we'll be on our way."

Micajah Jones laughed again. "I can't holler that loud." His smile shifted to Chancy and back to Uncle Will. "You're a mite late. Little Indiana ain't here."

Uncle Will's gaze sharpened. "Where is she, sir?"

"I don't rightly know. Day before yesterday — she picked up and run away."

12

The Strongbox

THE WORDS cracked like thunder across Chancy's mind. Wasn't that like Indiana? Gone! Run off! Hadn't she always been contrary? Confound it, she might have waited a day or two.

Even Uncle Will was taken by surprise. "Skipped out, did she?" he exploded. "By the eternal!"

Chancy's glance flashed back to Micajah Jones with withering hatred. Of course Indiana had cut and run. He'd have parted company from this infernal, weasel-eyed miser himself, and he wouldn't have waited four years.

"I expect she headed in the general direction of Erie County," Uncle Will said. "Chancy, we're standing in the wrong place."

Chancy went to the rear of the shed to fetch Calamity off the rung of a half-caned chair. He lowered his hand. Then he stopped short.

There, under a tangle of split cane, he saw a corn husk doll. It was tattered and yellowed with age. He knew that doll! He stared at the corn husk bonnet and the twisted arms and the long corn husk apron. The doll's painted blue eyes stared back at him.

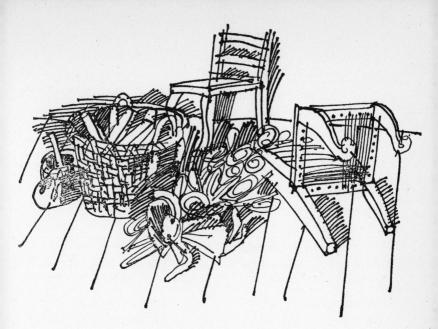

It was Tollie. It was Indiana's doll!

He turned. Micajah Jones was hanging the shotgun on pegs near the shed door. Chancy gave Uncle Will an earnest sign. When Uncle Will came over, he broke into a whisper. "Look! That's Indiana's doll."

"You certain, boy?"

"I'm dead certain. It's *Tollie*. Mama made that doll. Indiana wouldn't run off and leave Tollie behind! No more'n I would Pa's axe."

Uncle Will was scowling darkly. "Of course she wouldn't."

"Indiana must still be here!"

"Looks like she's been caning this very chair. And that crafty old fooler don't intend to give her up. That's why he was sending us off on a wild goose chase. He's got her and he aims to keep working her. Just pretend we don't suspect a thing. And let me handle the talk."

Chancy got hold of Calamity and followed Uncle Will to the shed doorway.

"We're obliged for your information, sir," Uncle Will said. "We'll start back in the morning. Too bad Indiana ran off that way. We've got her inheritance at the hotel and I'm anxious to turn it over to her."

Micajah Jones's eyebrows lifted like leaves caught on a wind. "Inheritance?"

"Yes, indeed. A strongbox left by her Pa back in Erie County before he went off to the war. We dug it up in the yard."

"A strongbox!"

"The stoutest strongbox you ever saw. Heavy, too."

"What's in it?"

Uncle Will hooked a thumb in the pocket of his calico vest. Chancy saw that tall tale look on his face. "No telling, sir. That strongbox belongs to Indiana. It was left to her. It wouldn't be right for us to open it."

"Heavy, you said?"

"Heavy as a brick."

"Buried, you said?"

"Three feet deep. It's beyond my imagining what's in it."

Micajah Jones was rising to the scent of riches like a fish to bait. He gave his chin a rasp with his long fingers. "A man wouldn't go to all that trouble to bury a brick, would he?"

Uncle Will ignored the question. "If she should turn up in the night, you'll find us at the Southern Hotel."

"She might at that," said Micajah Jones with a sudden laugh. "You know how it is with runaways. I reasoned she'd come home when she gets hungry enough."

"She'll be glad to get that box."

The chair maker cleared his throat. "I don't believe I caught your name," he said.

"Buckthorn," answered Uncle Will. "Will Buckthorn."

They left Micajah Jones cracking his knuckles thoughtfully in the doorway of the shed. They passed the persimmon tree and started toward the river. Chancy couldn't help taking a final backward glance at the house. The windows looked as empty as the eyes of a dead man. But then, at an upstairs window, he saw a face appear — a girl's face, pale as a ghost.

"Uncle Will!" he said.

But before Uncle Will could look the window darkened. The face was gone. Someone had drawn the shade.

Uncle Will's eyes narrowed. "You reckon it was Indiana?"

Chancy hesitated. He had had only a fleeting glimpse, but it was enough to rouse his anger all over again. "Bound to be. That man most likely has her locked up for some punishment."

"Most likely."

"Uncle Will, we can't leave her there!"

"We can't, but we're going to," Uncle Will said. "I dislike to walk away as much as you, Chancy. By ginger, I'd take a grand pleasure in breaking a hickory chair over that rascally man's head. But if we took Indiana he'd have the law on us before we got very far."

Chancy couldn't take his eyes off the upstairs window.

He could climb the persimmon tree and fetch Indiana in a minute.

But Uncle Will had him by the arm. "Come along. This thing has got to be done right. And the right thing is to walk away. Mark my word, before the night is done he'll turn Indiana over to us of his own free will. And I want his name on a piece of paper to prove it. If he intends to play the rascal he's met his match. I can play the grand rascal if the occasion calls for it. Before we're finished, Chancy — that man will bite himself."

On the way back Uncle Will picked up the strongbox with the broken hinge discarded among the leaves. He washed it clean in the river. "The box is sound enough," he said. "All it needs is a blacksmith." And when they found a blacksmith in Paducah, he said, "Braze the hinges so the box won't open, sir. In fact, seal the lid down all around. And while you're about it, sir — why, heat up an iron bar and wrap it around like rope. I want that box so almighty strong it would take Hercules twenty-four hours with a hammer and chisel to bang it open. We'll be back."

By dark Chancy and Uncle Will had got their supper, returned for the strongbox and sauntered to the Southern Hotel across from the wharf. It was a warm summer night and guests were seated outside, fanning themselves with folded newspapers and straw hats. Chancy and Uncle Will found chairs; there was nothing to do now but wait.

Uncle Will rested a foot on the strongbox and told stories of the war. Chancy could hardly keep his mind on what Uncle Will was saying. He expected at any moment to see Indiana and Micajah Jones loom out of the shadows.

Calamity went to sleep on Chancy's shoulder. The hours passed. "Oh, he'll be along, sure as a goose goes barefoot," Uncle Will said, and began telling stories about his travels through the Great Plains. It grew late and one by one the hotel guests retired to their rooms. Soon even the street and the wharf were deserted.

"Oh, he'll be along," Uncle Will said again. And then he added, "I declare, there he is now."

Chancy gave such a start he awoke Calamity on his shoulder. Micajah Jones was hurrying along under the yellow streetlights.

He was alone.

Chancy could barely conceal his disappointment, but

Uncle Will chuckled softly. "I calculated on it. He wants this empty strongbox first. He's come to outsmart us." Then Uncle Will raised his voice. "Evenin', Mr. Jones. You're looking for us, I believe."

The chair bottomer saw them and gave a lurch. "Why, indeed I am, sir," he said, smiling like the sun. "You're in luck. The girl has come home."

"I figured she would," said Uncle Will. "But I notice you didn't bring her along."

"Poor thing. She was all tuckered out from runnin' away."

"Naturally," said Uncle Will.

"Is that the strongbox?"

"It is. We don't like to let it out of our keep any more than we have to."

Micajah Jones cleared his throat and gazed hungrily at the box. "Must be a gracious plenty of things in there. Look at the iron around it! That box wasn't meant to be broken into, that's clear."

"Clear as well water," Uncle Will said.

The chair maker rasped his chin slowly. "You come for the girl, did you?"

"Indeed, sir."

"Then see here, we got business to discuss. You'd be surprised how much in arrears that girl is. I brought my account book with me. She ain't earned her keep by any means. I've got it all writ down in black and white. Why, just last month she broke my wife's best china teapot. That cost five dollars alone. And there's her feed and clothing — oh, it cost heaps to raise that girl." He paused, regarding Chancy with a cold eye, and then said, "Mr. Buckthorn, why don't we cross the way and talk it over? In private, so to speak."

"Chancy," said Uncle Will, "you and Calamity watch the strongbox. Guard it with your life, you hear?"

Chancy nodded. He didn't trust himself to say a word. The mere sight of the chair bottomer renewed his anger. It was clear now that Micajah Jones had spent the last hours scheming some way to cheat Indiana out of her inheritance. By dogs, he was in for a surprise!

Soon the two men were in the shadows of the wharf, deep in conversation beside a cotton bale. Chancy kept a foot on the strongbox, and watched. Fifteen or twenty minutes passed before Micajah Jones went loping away from the wharf. Uncle Will returned with his eyes blazing.

"Why that low-down, hang-jawed, weasel-eyed, long-necked skunk! When it comes to pure-bred meanness there's no doubt about it. That man's the devil red-hot from home."

Chancy prepared himself for the worst. "Won't he let Indiana go?"

"Not until we pay her debts first. He claims they amount to all of *two hundred and eighty-seven dollars!* It's right there in the account book, and not a word of truth between the covers! Of course, that's what he was doing all this time — making up and entering all those figures. Why, if Indiana ate all the food he charged up to her she'd have to eat ten meals a day."

Chancy was clinging to every word. "What did you say?"

"I told him we hadn't the money to pay her debts."

"What did he say to that?"

His anger discharged, Uncle Will suddenly broke into a

laugh. "Why, he said he'd take the strongbox in full payment. That's what he was after all along."

"Yes sir."

"I said — no, I couldn't do that, sir. It's Indiana's inheritance. And anyway, there might not be anything of value in the box. It wouldn't be fair to him. He said he'd be glad to chance it, sight unseen. Oh, he's sure it's a hoard of gold pieces. Still I kept saying no. He's been all this time wheedlin' and coaxin'. I finally gave in, providing he signed that account book paid in full — and wrote out a statement in his own hand makin' no further claims on Indiana's services."

"Did he go to fetch her?"

Uncle Will nodded. "Oh, he's out-foxed himself now. We're to meet halfway along the Tennessee in an hour."

The moon had risen and it shone in the Tennessee like a floating scrap of paper. Bullfrogs raised a steady thunder along the bank. Insects were so busy in the air that Chancy walked along with his mouth shut to keep from breathing them in.

When they came to a spreading bald cypress tree at the edge of the water, they stopped to wait. Chancy felt almost feverish with expectation. Calamity, roosting on his shoulder, was asleep with his head tucked under a wing.

Uncle Will puffed on a cigar. The minutes dragged on. Chancy shifted toward every sound, and finally Uncle Will straightened. "I believe they're coming."

Two figures took shape along the riverbank. There was no mistaking Micajah Jones even in the darkness. He seemed as long as a shadow, all neck and arms and legs. He was pulling a girl along by the arm. There were no braids to be seen; her hair was as loose and flowing as flax. But it was Indiana! Chancy could feel it. He was sure of it. And then he saw Tollie clutched in her hand.

"Here she is," Micajah Jones snapped without ceremony, drawing up at the cypress trees. "Where's the box?"

Uncle Will lifted the strongbox off the ground. "I'll thank you for the account book, sir, marked paid in full — and the words I asked for."

"Already done," said the chair bottomer. Uncle Will lit a match and examined the documents to his satisfaction. Then the exchange was made. Micajah Jones gave Indiana a final push. "Don't make any trouble, girl."

He turned her loose, wrapped an arm around the strongbox and loped away upriver. Hardly was his back to them

when Indiana gave Uncle Will a sharp kick to the leg and broke away — downriver.

Chancy was so taken by surprise it was a moment before he called out her name.

"Indiana!"

She didn't stop. Uncle Will was dancing about on one foot. Chancy rushed after her. Calamity awoke in midair and fluttered to the ground.

"Indiana!"

She was quick as a squirrel and Chancy almost lost sight of her in the tree shadows. She was heading toward Paducah and he raced after her. She could *run*. Her hair and skirts were flying in the pale moonlight.

"Wait up! It's me!"

Finally he gave a leap and brought her to the ground. Immediately, he felt as if he had tangled with a wildcat.

"You're gypsies!" she cried out. "I don't believe him! He's sold me to the raggle-taggle gypsies!"

"No! It's me, confound it! Your own brother!"

But she wasn't listening. She flailed out with her arms and caught him smartly across the ear. His head rang like a kettle and it was all he could do to hold her. Uncle Will caught up, favoring one leg, and pulled the two of them up by the arms.

"Here's a fine reunion," he laughed. "You two have hardly had time to say your howdies and you're a-scrapping already. Now see here, Indiana, we're not gypsies. Simmer down and meet your brother Chancy."

She gave a little gasp. Her eyes flashed up at him. But she was speechless. Or maybe, Chancy thought, she wasn't so all-fired glad to see him. Hadn't it taken him four years to come fetch her?

"I declare, Indiana," he said finally. "You sure can run. I was lucky to come in last."

Suddenly a smile flickered across her face. "My own brother Chancy? All the way from Erie County?"

She had forgot all about being mad at him. By dogs!

"It's nothing to bawl about," Chancy said quickly. He was sure her eyes were dewing up.

"I'm not bawling."

"And don't faint away, either."

"I'm not about to."

"I reckon we can shake hands, though."

"*Howdy,* Chancy," she said at last, shaking his hand.

"Howdy, Indiana," he replied. "This is our Uncle Will."

She turned and gave her head an astonished tilt. "Uncle Will?"

"The war didn't get him, and neither did the Indians."

"Uncle Will!"

Will Buckthorn gave her a hug and a kiss and lifted her into the air. "Let me study you. I declare, you've got your mother's own eyes — bright and shiny as the morning star. But you kick like a mule, Indiana. I swear you do."

"I'm *sorry,* Uncle Will."

"By ginger, we're together now, the three of us. You won't ever have to go back to Micajah Jones. And we won't rest until we've hunted up Mirandy and little Jamie."

Uncle Will found Tollie nearby and Calamity came screeching along, looking for Chancy. It seemed to Chancy

he needed something to give Indiana. He lifted Calamity on the back of his hand and turned.

"You never saw such a smart bird, Indiana. I named him Calamity, but you can change that if you want to. He's yours."

Indiana accepted the chick joyously, and Chancy felt a glow of delight. Calamity walked up her arm to her shoulder. "Calamity," she said softly. "I wouldn't *think* of changing it."

Soon they started back for town, talking and laughing all the way. Indiana had to skip along to keep up. Uncle Will decided that they ought to treat themselves to a real hotel room. He lifted his slouch hat, set Calamity on his head and replaced his hat. Then the three of them walked into the Southern Hotel and Uncle Will registered. They were given rooms overlooking the river. Chancy had never been inside a hotel before and neither had Indiana. And neither had Calamity. The chick roosted for the night on Indiana's brass bedstead.

The raft ought to turn up along the river the next day, and they could be on their way

13

The Letter

"INDIANA, you don't look like you've had a square meal in four years," Uncle Will said early the next morning. "You're so thin I believe you could fall through a stovepipe without getting sooty. Let's eat."

Chancy was anxious to leave Paducah behind. He expected to see Micajah Jones come charging down the street at any moment, but no doubt he was still struggling to open the strongbox.

After breakfast, Uncle Will took a second look at Indiana's tattered cotton dress and they marched into the nearest mercantile store. When they came marching out, Indiana was resplendent in new white petticoats and a crisp blue flowered dress. Her cheeks were flushed with excitement. She couldn't pass her reflection in the store windows without stopping; she hardly knew herself.

"By dogs," Chancy said, losing patience at last. "You'll bust your eyesight, Indiana, if you look at yourself one more pesky time."

Nevertheless, she paused at the next window. "I declare, I may be plain as poverty," she sighed, "but don't I look *clean*, though?"

"Plain!" Uncle Will exploded. "Who ever told you you were plain? Why, you're pretty as a June rabbit."

She gave a skip and abandoned her reflections with a smile. She seemed to shed the unhappiness of the last four years together with the ragged cotton dress. It had surprised Chancy to find Indiana almost as tall as he, even though she was a year younger. But it had surprised him even more when he discovered, among the counter signs at the mercantile store, that she didn't know A from B. Indiana couldn't read.

At the same time, she noticed that Chancy was able to read everything in sight, and she was deeply impressed. Now she said, "You're perishin' smart, Chancy."

"Readin' don't amount to much," he answered. "It's getting downright common. A regiment of folks can read."

"I can't."

"Didn't old Micajah make you go to school?"

"Make me? He wouldn't allow me!" She made a wry face. "He claimed learnin' was bad for girls. Makes their hair fall out."

"What infernal rubbish," Uncle Will scowled. "Chancy, you show your sister how to read. And a little writin' won't hurt either."

"Me?" said Chancy. "Me! I'm no schoolmaster!"

"Oh, please!" Indiana cried. "I won't be any trouble. I promise! I'll do everything you say. Even a girl ought to be able to write her own name, oughten she?"

Chancy shrugged, but secretly he felt a surge of pride. Indiana looked up to him, and it pleased him. "I reckon I could do *that* much," he said. "I'll have you scratching out Indiana Dundee quicker'n you can scald a cat."

"I declare, Chancy," Indiana said. "You're *perishin'* clever!"

After checking out of the hotel they walked along the dusty levee to wait for the log raft to round the bend. Indiana was careful not to get her dress dirty. They found a shady elm to sit under, but all the while Chancy couldn't help keeping an eye out for Micajah Jones.

"Oh, I expect he's just about got the strongbox split open," said Uncle Will. "If you hear a howl that'll be him taking a bite out of himself."

Uncle Will's thoughts kept returning to Mirandy and little Jamie. They might be anywhere west of the Mississippi and that covered almost too much territory to contemplate. He wouldn't admit it to Chancy and Indiana, but it could take years to track them down.

It had caught Indiana by surprise to learn that Mirandy and Jamie were no longer living in Erie County. Now, for the first time, Indiana thought to mention that she had once had a letter from them.

"A letter!" said Chancy.

"A letter!" said Uncle Will.

Chancy leaped to his feet. "What did it say?"

Uncle Will was on his feet too. "When did it arrive? Where was it from?"

These questions, coming so swiftly, made Indiana jump. After a moment of earnest thought, she said, "It was early last fall — I remember the persimmons were ripe on the tree."

"Hang the persimmons!" said Chancy. "What did the letter say?"

She took a long breath and answered in a distressed tone. "I don't know, Chancy."

"Didn't you read it?"

"I *told* you I can't!"

Chancy was abashed. "You could have got old Micajah to read it off to you."

"You don't think I'd let *him,* do you? Or any of *them* at the house."

"Indiana," said Uncle Will. "How do you know that letter came from Mirandy and little Jamie?"

"Mister Micajah said so when he handed it to me. He said it was a letter from my kin. Oh, I used to sit up in the persimmon tree studyin' it from beginning to end many a time, Uncle Will — imagining all the nice things it said. It was the prettiest writin' you ever saw, full of curlicues, like birds a-frolickin' through the air."

"Hang the birds a-frolickin' through the air!" Chancy exclaimed. "Where's the letter now? Did you keep it?"

Indiana was beginning to feel quite badgered. "Of course I kept it. I kept it hid up in the persimmon tree — the limb that hangs near my window. And you needn't look at me that way, Chancy Dundee. I'd as soon let the moon shine in my mouth as leave that letter behind. But Mister Micajah pulled me out of the house so quick I hardly had time to fetch Tollie." And then she said, "What's so precious important about that letter, anyway?"

"It didn't come from Erie County," Uncle Will answered. "That letter was from out West. Miss Russell took Mirandy and little Jamie with her more than a year ago, and she must have written it. No one's blaming you. But if we had that letter we could set off straight as a beeline and find them."

"Mercy," Indiana whispered.

Uncle Will began buttoning up his yellow vest. "No use standing around talking. I'm going to climb that persimmon tree and get the letter. You two stay here and watch for the raft."

Uncle Will disappeared over the top of the levee and Chancy was left alone with Indiana. The thought of Uncle Will returning to the house filled Chancy with foreboding. He sat in the dust and stared at the river.

After a long silence Indiana said, "I'm desperate sorry, Chancy."

Chancy nodded, but he didn't feel like talking.

Indiana gave him several sidelong glances. "You're sittin' there looking older'n a tree," she said finally. "If you want to holler at me, go ahead."

He said nothing.

"You want Calamity back?" she murmured.

He took a slow breath and turned to her. "I never met anyone who did things so contrary, Indiana. You should have collared *somebody* to read you that letter."

"That's so."

"I vow, you're so contrary if you fell in the river you'd float upstream."

"That's the perishin' truth, Chancy."

Chancy closed his eyes and lay back with his hands folded under his head. "You just peel your eyesight for that raft."

"It won't get by me. Don't you worry. And if I'm contrary again you pick up a stick and give me a thrashing."

After a while Indiana puffed a strand of hair out of her eyes. "Did you ever know it so hot?"

"I scarcely noticed," Chancy said. "Down in Texas it really gets hot. You have to prime yourself to spit."

"How do you know?"

"Uncle Will told me. He's been most everywhere. He's seen the Pacific Ocean."

"Gracious," Indiana said.

"You want Calamity to fan your face?"

"I'd be more'n grateful!"

He called Calamity from the top of the levee and showed Indiana how to manage the trick. But Calamity was more interested in pecking at the buttons on Indiana's dress than in performing. At long last the trick worked.

"My," Indiana said. "Calamity beats up a powerful gust. Don't it feel cool, though?"

"He needs a mite more practice."

"I'll practice." And then Indiana said, "What do you reckon we'll do after we find Mirandy and Jamie?"

"They're not found yet."

"*If*, then."

Chancy hadn't really thought that far ahead. Uncle Will sometimes talked of finding a place to roost, but Chancy chose not to mention that. "I expect we'll just keep movin' around, seeing places. That's the way Uncle Will is. He's a coming-and-going man, you know. Strong as a buffalo, too. Why, he can pull a wagon with his teeth."

"Mercy. Fan me, Calamity."

Chancy picked up a stick and Indiana shot him a fearful glance.

"Did I say something contrary?" she muttered.

Chancy ignored her and scratched a mark in the dirt. "This is an A," he said.

She saw that he wasn't going to thrash her after all. "An A what?" she asked.

"An A! You want to learn your letters, don't you? You got to start with A. You don't expect to start with zed, do you?"

"What does zed look like?"

He scratched out a Z beside the A and she studied the markings in the dust. "I do favor the look of that zed," she admitted.

"But the alphabet starts at the other end. It starts with A."

"Why? Fan me, Calamity."

Chancy threw down the stick and began watching the river again. He wasn't cut out for schoolmastering, that was clear. Indiana picked up the stick and began making A's. She made them in all sizes, from a foot tall down to an inch or so. After ten minutes she had the ground around them covered. He tried to ignore her, but then he began to wonder if he could say the alphabet backwards and finally he decided there was no law against starting with zed. It would serve Indiana right.

"Forget all those A's," he said. "We're going to start from the hindmost end, since you're naturally so contrary." He took the stick from her and once more made a Z.

"Don't it look like a duck floating along in the water," Indiana said. "Oh, I like that zed."

She worked her way along the bank of the levee making Z's by the flock, and then he started her on Y's and X's.

Calamity followed, pecking and cheeping at the end of the stick.

Before long they had backed through the alphabet as far as Q, and Chancy had to admit that Indiana was quick to learn. Finally, she stood gazing at her scratchings with a glow of pride. "What does ZYXWVUTSRQ spell?" she asked.

"It doesn't spell anything."

She was crestfallen. "Not even cat?"

"No."

"Dog?"

"Nothing."

"What *good* is it, then?"

"What good is it?" Chancy felt challenged. "Why, those are powerful letters."

"They appear kind of triflin' to me."

"Trifling! I know some mighty fine words that would wither up and die without those letters."

"Name one."

Chancy lay back and peered at the sky through the elm leaves. "Tree, for a start. Noah Webster himself couldn't spell tree without the T and the R."

"Run!"

"Oh, you couldn't begin to spell run."

"Run quick!"

Chancy had been too occupied to detect the first alarm in her voice. But now he rolled to his feet and saw Calamity flying over the top of the levee and Micajah Jones with a shotgun looming against the sky.

As suddenly as flushed birds they bolted. Indiana snatched up Tollie and Calamity raced along behind.

"Stop, you schemin' brats!" shouted the chair bottomer. "Where's that man who bamboozled me!"

Nothing short of a hole in the ground would have stopped Chancy. And Indiana was racing along in a flutter of new petticoats.

"Stop! You hear me!"

Chancy expected buckshot to come roaring through the air after them. Still they ran. They leaped a tree root, one after the other, and raced on. Then, so suddenly that he could hardly believe his eyes, Chancy saw the log raft drifting slowly around the bend.

"Captain Harpe!" he yelled. "Billy Arkansas!"

At that distance his voice barely carried and the raftsman paid no attention to him. Then the shotgun boomed and Chancy's heart jumped a mile. It astonished him that he was not shot full of holes. And neither was Indiana. With a quick backward glance he saw Micajah Jones sprawled in the dust. He had stumbled on the tree root and the shotgun had exploded wild.

But the report carried to the raft and did them a service. The raftsmen were now peering their way.

Chancy began waving his arms. "Billy Arkansas! It's us! Captain Harpe! Poosh Johnson! We're here!"

Captain Harpe gave a wave and then the raft began to move like a crab toward the Kentucky shore.

But Micajah Jones was on his feet again and was reloading the gun as he loped along. "Indiana! You're a-comin' home!"

The boom of the shotgun had frightened Calamity out of a dozen feathers. The chick was suddenly *ahead* of Chancy and Indiana, its feet barely touching the ground.

There was hardly a breath left between the three of them as the raft came angling toward shore. Chancy caught Calamity by the feet and began wading out through the shallows. But Indiana stopped short.

"My new dress!" she gasped.

"Hang your dress!" Chancy shouted, and yanked her by the arm into the water.

They were waist deep when Billy Arkansas reached them with a long sweep oar. They clung to the broad pine blade, Chancy and Indiana, Calamity and Tollie. Swinging the oar on the headblock, Billy Arkansas gave them a swift ride through the air and set them gently down on the raft.

"Hoolah-haw!" laughed Captain Harpe, raising his brown bowler hat to Indiana. "Looks like we plucked you from the very jaws of mischief. What's that durn fool shoutin' and shootin' about?"

Chancy explained as quickly as he could and Captain Harpe broke into guffaws. For the first time Chancy stopped to realize that Uncle Will and Micajah Jones had clearly missed each other at the house.

The chair bottomer was now standing at the water's edge with the shotgun drawn up at his shoulder.

"You, there! Put that girl ashore!"

Captain Harpe gave Chancy a nod. "You take the little lady into the doghouse. Billy! That gentleman out there needs the arch taken out of his back."

Again Micajah Jones's voice floated across the still water. "I aim to shoot!"

Billy Arkansas answered with glee, uncovering his squirrel gun from a tarpaulin. "So do I!"

The squirrel gun! Chancy's eyes widened. If Billy Arkansas had his squirrel gun it meant he had caught up with Colonel Plugg. Chancy rushed to the doghouse.

There, propped in a corner, stood the four-pound axe. Chancy's heart was beating wildly. Slowly, he wrapped his fingers around the worn black cherry handle, and tossed Indiana a smile. "You stay put."

He ducked outside to the roar of a gun.

He flattened himself against the creaking logs. A rattle of buckshot fell against the black chimney pipe, which fell apart and went clattering along the deck.

"Answer back!" Captain Harpe growled.

"Can't," Billy Arkansas protested. "There's some fool coming over the levee right behind him!"

Chancy raised his head and saw that it was Uncle Will.

Micajah Jones was still hurling threats. "That girl's a runaway! You hear! Turn her loose or I'll buckshot you proper!"

The chair bottomer wasn't aware that he had company until he felt a tap on the shoulder. He gave a turn, his jaw fell slack, and Chancy saw Uncle Will snatch the shotgun out of his hands.

Unhurried, he bent the long barrel around his raised knee as if it were a sapling, and returned it.

"Mercy," Indiana whispered from the doorway of the doghouse. "He bent that gun into a U, didn't he?"

The helpless anger in Micajah Jones's face glowed up red as fire. The raft kept drifting in until Uncle Will stepped on an oar and walked aboard without so much as getting his feet wet.

He turned and lifted his hat to the chair bottomer. "Good day, sir. Let me remind you I've papers in my pocket to show you tried to scheme an orphan girl out of her inheritance. You're lucky to get off with a bent shotgun. The next time you try to get the best of some poor soul, remember that a cat looks big until a dog comes along."

Captain Harpe began to chuckle. "Ain't he a sight? I declare, that man looks mad enough to bite himself!"

Chancy showed Uncle Will the axe and Captain Harpe quickly told how they had come upon Colonel Plugg in the next town along the river. "The danged fool was sound asleep in the best hotel! Oh, I wish you could have been there to see it. Billy snatched him bareheaded, and then I kicked him so high I doubt if he'll be seen again in our lifetime!"

Chancy grinned. Colonel Plugg had got his comeuppance. But did Uncle Will find Indiana's letter?

"Why, I near forgot," he laughed, drawing the wrinkled envelope from his coat pocket. Indiana and Chancy gathered around while he read it in a low, quiet voice.

Dearest Indiana,

Mirandy and Jamie want to send their love. I am writing this for them. We want you to join us if you can. If this letter reaches you and you are free to leave Paducah, will you let us know? I will send you traveling money. We cannot find a trace of your brother Chancy. Perhaps you know where he is.

Do write. We are living in Sun Dance, Kansas, not far from Abilene, and there is plenty of room for you. Do come to us!

Your loving,

Mirandy
Jamie
(and Callie Russell)

Uncle Will looked up smiling. "You were right, Indiana. Miss Russell does write like birds a-frolicking through the air. Odd she didn't sign her new married name. Young'uns, it looks like we're headed for Kansas!"

14

The Liars' Contest

SUMMER LIGHTNING flickered in the western sky. Stripped to his shirtsleeves, Uncle Will spent long hours at a forward raft oar. Captain Harpe stood with one boot off and his toes bare while Indiana darned his sock. Now he peered at the darkening sky. "It wouldn't surprise me if we reached the Mississip' in time for a pour-down, and that won't be long."

Uncle Will called to Chancy and told him to pack the wheelbarrow. "We'll be getting off at Cairo and head for the Great Plains."

Chancy hopped to it. He was anxious to see the Mississippi. Uncle Will said it was almost brown as tobacco juice, but Chancy would believe that when he saw it with his own eyes.

The flock of chicks wandered over the raft as if it were a barnyard. A roll of thunder sent them jumping about for cover. Soon Chancy had the wheelbarrow stowed with the axe, the wedges, the bedrolls and Uncle Will's clocks and belongings. He would be sorry to leave Captain Harpe and Billy Arkansas and the others. But once on the Mississippi the raft would follow the current south. They must go west.

Gazing at Uncle Will, Captain Harpe clasped his hands forlornly behind his back.

"You're mighty welcome if you folks want to stay on," he said. "I do hate to lose a bully raftsman. I'll pay you a dollar a day to buck that oar to New Orleans with us."

"That's a temptin' offer," Uncle Will smiled. "But New Orleans happens to be in the wrong direction."

"Wrong direction! Why, sir, your ignorance of geography is astounding! Kansas sidles right spang alongside of Louisiana these days. I'm surprised you didn't hear about it."

"By the eternal!" said Uncle Will.

"I hope I may be skinned if it ain't the solemn truth. Just after the war a government surveyin' party went out there and found Kansas missing. Turned out a tornado had come along and rolled up the whole state like a carpet and laid it down, pretty as you please, in the lower right-hand corner of Texas."

"I do recall, now that you mention it," said Uncle Will. "But I reckon you didn't hear about the Mexican jumping beans."

"Jumping beans? What's that got to do with simple geography!"

"Why, them Kansans didn't know any better than to use 'em for stock feed. I'd like to see you eat a bushel of jumping beans and keep your feet on the ground. Cows, chickens, cats and dogs were soon leapin' about in the air like fleas on a red-hot stove. Folks tied 'em down and that was a mistake. That livestock was soon uprooting trees and fenceposts and the scenery itself. In three months, when the dust cleared, Kansas had hopped right back where it used to be, although they did have to leave their hills behind. If you doubt my word, you come along and see for yourself. If you don't find Kansas flat as a skillet you can call me a liar."

Captain Harpe gave a large sigh and Indiana handed him his wool sock. "Good as new," she said.

"Thank you, little lady." He sat on a keg and pulled on the sock. "This raft just won't be home with you folks gone."

Before long Cairo crept out of the trees on the Illinois bank. With dusty levees guarding against high waters, it stood like a walled city at the meeting place of the two rivers. The raft surged along past steamboats and tugs, their smoking funnels darkening the low and thundering sky.

And then, dead ahead, the two rivers collided.

Chancy and Indiana rushed forward along the string of logs and gazed at the great river broadside in their path.

"By dogs," said Chancy. "Almost brown as tobacco juice."

"Don't that bang all!" Indiana exclaimed.

Soon, under their feet, the clear Ohio assaulted the muddy Mississippi like a battering ram. The two rivers tangled, the logs plunged and climbed, and the raft went bounding over a swirling battlefield. The current carried them southward and before long the duel of rivers lay behind and the Ohio was a thing of tatters and streamers.

Chancy scooped up a handful of the muddy river and Indiana did the same. They took a taste, and Chancy made a face. "Curls your tongue."

"Don't it, though!"

Boys in skiffs made toward the raft and held up rusty sabers and minié balls and old army guns — relics of naval battles that had been fought on the river.

Chancy silently looked over war pieces while Captain Harpe tried to shoo the skiffs away. Chancy wished he had an old army gun, and glanced at Uncle Will, but he knew it was beyond his having.

Cairo was dropping away behind and Uncle Will finally shipped his thirty-foot oar. He pulled on his calico vest and his frock coat. "I gave you a hand over the rough water. We'll be gettin' off now, Cap."

Captain Harpe peered at the sky and twiddled his thumbs. "Oh, I couldn't put you ashore in this rain. I wouldn't do that to a dog."

"It ain't rainin' yet," Uncle Will said.

"Will be afore we can edge over to the bank."

"A little wet won't hurt us." Uncle Will pushed back his hat. "You going to make us swim ashore?"

"Well, sir, if you insist on being foolhardy I can't stop you. But there's a right smart current under us and we might not be able to stop until we get to New Orleans."

A crash of thunder broke overhead, the rain came rushing down, splattering like grapes, and almost everyone made a dive for the doghouse — including the chickens. The raft was just scraping past the funnel of a sunken boat. It stood out of the water like a tree stump. Billy Arkansas and Hawg Pewitt and Poosh Johnson got lines around it and made the raft fast. Then they joined the others in the doghouse to wait out the storm.

"Listen to it deluge!" Captain Harpe howled gleefully. "Why, sir, the roads'll be so muddy it'll take you a month to take three steps. You change your mind and come along with us."

Another bang of thunder shook the doghouse. The flock of chicks hit the roof and fluttered down on heads, shoulders and knees.

Uncle Will slipped Chancy and Indiana a sly wink, cleared his throat and hooked a thumb in his vest pocket. "Captain Harpe," he said, "this rain will hardly last long enough to wet down the dust, and you're going to have to set us ashore."

"I declare, sir, you try a man's hospitality."

"But I intend to make you a sporting offer to pass the time. I don't mean to cast aspersions on your honesty, sir, but I have heard you string up a bunch of nonsense now and again. I have some talent in that direction myself, sir. I dislike to brag, but when it comes to tamperin' with the truth, I reckon I can hold my own against you."

Captain Harpe's eyes glistened from the depths of his brow and beard. "Are you proposin' a contest?"

"As long as we're stuck here in the rain," Will Buckthorn nodded. "If I can't stretch the truth further than you — why, we'll come along to New Orleans with you. Let the boys be the judge. But if you lose — why, then you put us ashore and wish us luck on our travels. What's more, *I promise to out-whopper you in no more than seven words.*"

"Seven words!" Chancy gasped.

"*Seven words!*" Indiana exclaimed.

"Seven words!" Captain Harpe grinned with delight. *"Hoolah-haw!* Boys, give me lung room. The contest is in session. Any preference as to subject, sir?"

"None at all," answered Uncle Will. Indiana turned pale and Chancy tried to reassure her with a glance. She didn't know Uncle Will as well as he did. She didn't know what a grand rascal he was! And of course, they were only fooling about New Orleans — or so Chancy hoped.

"Well, sir," said Captain Harpe, "since we're sittin' here on the muddy Mississip' I'll tell you how wrong folks can be in the things they say about it. They'll tell you it's too thick to drink and too thin to plow, but that's an outright slander. I ought to know. I done both."

"Shucks," said Billy Arkansas. "I drunk it myself."

Captain Harpe shot him an eye like a fighting cock. "You ever plow it?"

"Reckon not."

Captain Harpe squared his shoulders. "I was running logs from the pineries up north a few years back. Let me see, that must have been in the summer of eighteen and sixty. You remember what a dry year that was. Why, the old Mississip' near turned to mud. It ran slower'n molasses in winter and just as thick. You couldn't raft logs in that stuff even if you was to lie about it. So I decided I'd farm it. I got the loan of some hogs and turned them loose in the river. They went rootin' and wallowin' through the mud, plowing up the old Mississip' for me. Then I came along on mudshoes and planted twenty acres of corn and twenty acres in wheat."

"What are mudshoes?" asked Hawg Pewitt.

"You durned fool, what do you think they are? They're

shoes for walkin' on mud. As I was sayin', that Mississip' river farm just meandered along in the sun, slow as molasses headin' south. I moseyed along with it, weeding and scaring off blackbirds. Well, sir, by time we got to Red Wing, that corn was a foot high. I hope I never see daylight again if that's not the gospel truth. When we come through Dubuque that cornfield was shoulder high. Folks come out to look at it. Soon word spread up and down the river, and they used to meet me with brass bands. Oh, it was a glorious time. The corn was in tassel before we reached St. Louis and the wheat was trailin' along behind pretty as you please. Sometimes that farm of mine was twisted into an S around the bends. Of course, that corn and wheat field was on the move day and night and I had to hang out running lights. By the time we edged past Memphis the corn was getting plump on the stalks and the wheat was tall as a fence. It looked to me like I could start harvesting about the time we reached Natchez. I was up at chicken-crow that morning, and I don't mind telling you that folks was lined up thick along both banks of the river to cheer me on. Bands began to play. The sun-ball came up hot as fire — turned out to be one of the *hottest* days of the century. I had just started pickin' corn when I noticed black smoke risin' from below the next bend. A steamboat was comin' on like a wildcat was chasin' it. It wasn't a wildcat, it was *another* steamboat — they was racin'. Well, sir, I yelled and waved my arms, but those boats weren't goin' to slow down for man or beast. The first one went thrashin' up my river farm, the paddle wheel shuckin' and shellin' the corn before my very eyes. The second boat got into my wheat field and filled the air white as fog. But it wasn't fog. It was flour

—fine milled, too. Well, sir, it was a sad sight, but not for long. Did I tell you it was a blisterin' hot mornin'? Why, the old Mississip' was steamin' like a skillet. When the corn and flour hit the river they began to fry a golden brown. Sir, *those were the bulliest corn fritters I ever ate!*"

There was a moment's stillness, and then laughter erupted in the doghouse. The chickens jumped again and traded perches. Uncle Will seemed to enjoy the tale most of all, and despite herself a chuckle slipped between Indiana's teeth. Chancy's heart was sinking. By dogs, that was a gollywhopper, and he felt miserable.

The rain was slackening off. Captain Harpe, his face aglow with impending victory, began to polish his hard hat with his sleeve. "Well, sir, you think you can match that?"

"I intend to better it."

"In *seven* words?"

"No more."

The raftsmen looked with piteous smiles at Uncle Will, who remained the soul of confidence. He lit a cigar and not a sound stirred in the doghouse. He buttoned his vest — Chancy thought he would die waiting. Then Uncle Will cleared his throat, leaned forward and looked Captain Harpe squarely in the eye. "Cap," he said, "that was as tall a story as I ever heard. Now here's mine. *I believe every yawhawin' word you said!*"

Twenty minutes later the travelers parted. Captain Harpe paid Chancy seventy-five cents for the flock of chicks and Uncle Will a dollar for every day he had worked aboard the raft. They exchanged farewells, and Chancy began to push the wheelbarrow through the mud. The sun was out, the Missouri bank began to steam, and they started on their way to Kansas.

15

The Great Plains

THEY WALKED all the way to St. Louis. They arrived early in August, in the sunniest of spirits and with a jangle of money in their pockets. Uncle Will had sold two clocks along the way, shingled a barn roof, and picked up a day's work here and there as a tramp printer. Passing from one river town to the next, Chancy had chopped stovewood and Indiana had bottomed chairs. She had also learned to write her name, scratching it a thousand times between Cairo and St. Louis.

With the extra money they had made, they treated themselves to steamboat tickets and traveled in style up the Missouri River to Kansas City. Indiana had woven a cage out of split cane and carried Calamity as grandly as a parrot.

Pushing the wheelbarrow before them, they walked from the boat landing straight to the Kansas Pacific train depot. Chancy had never ridden a train before and neither had Indiana. While Uncle Will bought tickets they gazed at the engine, belching smoke from its funnel and hissing steam like a great serpent.

Indiana was hesitant about the journey ahead. "That thing don't look entirely friendly," she whispered.

The bell began to clang. Uncle Will heaved the wheelbarrow into the baggage car and hustled Chancy and Indiana aboard.

They settled themselves on hard wooden seats in the immigrant car. It was the cheapest fare, but they would arrive in Abilene late that afternoon, and that beat walking. From there they would have to make their way as best they could to Sun Dance.

A potbellied stove stood at either end of the car and spittoons were lined up along the aisle like a double row of brass buttons. It all seemed immensely grand to Chancy and Indiana. They found themselves in a jolly company of settlers, poor adventurers, land seekers, ex-soldiers and entire families heading west to make new lives for themselves.

The train was soon rattling out across the open prairie. Here and there a windmill stood like a sunflower on the horizon. Smoke came swirling back from the engine, and despite the heat the passengers were forced to close their windows.

They rushed on, mile after mile, hour after hour, with the hard wooden seats under them reverberating to the *clickety-cut clickety-cut* of the wheels. Chancy spent a good deal of time polishing his buckeye. The towns they passed grew smaller and smaller until there was nothing to be seen but a few weathered shacks and a water tower gleaming in the sun. They hurtled past a covered wagon train lumbering west. As the afternoon wore on the horizon seemed to recede and the sky grew huge and overwhelming. Now and then the engine jerked to a stop as if to catch its fiery breath and took on wood. They got out to stretch their legs, but soon the train was on its way again. Indiana was sure her teeth would come rattling out like shelled corn before they reached Abilene.

Abilene was only a few miles off when Chancy, gazing through the window, said, "Redskins!"

Gazing back, and almost close enough to touch, stood three Indians mounted on ponies beside the iron rails.

"Mercy," Indiana whispered, slipping down in her seat. Civilization seemed suddenly far behind.

Dust was blowing off the Great Plains when the Kansas Pacific, which didn't reach the Pacific but hoped to some day, set them down in the booming new cow town of Abilene. A steady lowing of cattle was carried on the wind. Texas longhorns, waiting to be shipped east to the stockyards, were grazing in huge herds on the surrounding prairie. Texas cowboys were lounging everywhere along the dust-blown main street.

Chancy could hardly believe his eyes. Here were men in wide-brimmed hats and buckskin shirts and guns hanging from their cartridge belts. Cowboys! The jingle and jangle of spurs chimed in the wind. Chancy felt set down at the edge of the world. Everywhere he looked stood men unlike any he'd ever seen — long-haired scouts, horse soldiers with yellow stripes down their legs, mule skinners, and even a savage or two with an eagle feather tucked in his hair. Indiana was agog. It was like an outdoor costume ball.

Uncle Will himself was amazed. "How the place has

grown!" he said. "Last time I was in Kansas you couldn't find Abilene if you were standing in the middle of it."

He led them across the tracks to the Drovers' Cottage, where he signed the register and they had supper. In the crowded dining room cattle owners and cattle buyers bargained over the herds that were waiting on bed-ground for miles around. And if the talk wasn't about the price of longhorns, it was about jayhawkers.

"What in tarnation are jayhawkers?" said Chancy, who had been so busy looking and listening that he had hardly said a word since arriving in Abilene.

"Outlaws," Uncle Will answered. "A ragtag and bobtail breed of men left over from the war. They roam around the countryside plundering and shooting folks as if the war

never ended. A bad lot — with rewards on their heads, most of them."

The name that seemed on everyone's tongue was Seven-Eyes Smith. He and his gang had tried to rustle a herd of cattle to the south, but the drovers had fought them off.

When Uncle Will rose in the morning, he surprised Chancy by digging deep in his carpetbag and buckling on a gun belt. He had owned a six-shooter all along.

"By dogs!" Chancy said. He had taken a fancy to the Great Plains already. He wouldn't mind growing up in a buckskin shirt and wearing spurs on his boots. If Uncle Will decided to roost in Kansas that would suit him fine.

They went around to the livery stable, rented a buckboard and loaded their possessions. They sat close together on the spring seat, with Calamity and Tollie, and started out for Sun Dance, a few hours to the southwest.

With Mirandy and little Jamie now so close Indiana couldn't sit still. "Stop your squirming," Chancy said finally.

"Can't. I've got the all-over fidges. Do you reckon they'll remember us?"

"Not likely. They were just young'uns when we left."

"Oh, I don't think Miss Russell would let them forget you," Uncle Will said.

The wind had died away in the night and there wasn't a scrap of cloud in the wide blue sky. The buckboard passed longhorns and cow camps by the mile. The prairie spreading outside Abilene had become a huge holding ground.

Uncle Will shook his head at the wonder of it all. "By the eternal, it looks like all Texas is camped right here in Kansas!"

Late in the morning the buckboard crossed a creek and suddenly Indiana gave a yelp. "Look there! That man's fixin' to drown a litter of kittens."

Uncle Will pulled up on the reins and then he swung the buckboard along the shallow creek. The man was a short, squat cowboy with legs bent like barrel staves. He was about to lower a lumpy, mewling sack when Uncle Will pulled up.

"Howdy," he said, shoving back his hat. "Would those be felines you've got there?"

"No, sir," answered the cowman. "They're cats, and I'm fixin' to return them to their Maker. One ugly old meow around the chuck wagon is bother enough."

"Are you the chef?"

"No, sir. I'm the cook. Over with the Lazy Q outfit. We're holdin' our beeves until we can get twenty-five dollars a head. You a cattle buyer?"

"No, sir. I merely stopped to see if you'd let me have a look at those cats. I'd like to know what time it is so I can set my clock."

"What time it is?" The cook's eyes narrowed. "What in blazes has a cat got to do with settin' your clock?"

"Why, cats keep splendid time, sir," said Uncle Will, stepping down from the wagon. He opened the sack and pulled up a tiger kitten that barely filled his hand. He studied it a minute and said, "It appears to be eighteen minutes to eleven — exactly."

The cook's weathered face wrinkled at the eyes. "Stranger, you mean to stand there and tell me you can look at a cat and read the time?"

"Certainly, sir," said Uncle Will. He opened his carpetbag, found the last of his clocks and set the hands at eighteen minutes to eleven.

"Well, that beats all!" said the cook. "How do you do that?"

"Experience," said Uncle Will, hooking a thumb in his vest pocket. "Practice, and more practice. It's all in the darks of the eyes — the way they widen and shrink with the daylight. If you study a kitten's eyes long enough you get so you can just about hit the time on the head. I'm never more'n a minute or two off."

"Fry me brown!" said the cook. "Could I do that?"

"I wouldn't be surprised."

"Practice, you say."

"And more practice."

"I believe I might hold out one of these meows. Won't the boys jump out of their boots when they see me tell time!"

"It's none of my business," said Uncle Will, "but I'd advise you to hang onto the whole litter. I've known cats to run slow and run fast. After you get the hang of it, you'll know which one makes the best timepiece."

"Why, I'm obliged to you, hoss. Just study the darks of the eye, do you?"

Uncle Will nodded. "At first you'll need to check cat time against your timepiece — while you're learning, I mean. You do own a watch, don't you?"

The cook gave out a great sigh. "Drat it! Until this minute the only time I reckoned was daytime and nighttime, and I never needed a watch for that. What'll you take for that clock?"

Uncle Will shook his head. "Oh, I couldn't let that go. It's the only one I've got."

"Well, see here, hoss. I'll give you one of these cats and you won't *need* your clock. Take your pick. And I'll pay you what that clock's worth, as long as it ain't over ten dollars."

Uncle Will thought it over. "I sorely hate to part with that clock, but I reckon you need it more than I do. Ten dollars will do fine. Indiana, which one of them kittens takes your eye?"

She leaped joyously from the wagon and went through the sack. In no time at all the bargain was completed. Uncle Will gave the reins a snap. The camp cook went happily

on his way with the lumpy, mewling sack and the last of Uncle Will's timepieces.

"Reckon that puts me out of the clock business," said Will Buckthorn.

"Can you really tell time from a cat's eyes?" Indiana asked.

"I don't know," he answered. "I never tried it before.' And on they rode toward Sun Dance.

16

Sun Dance

CLOUDS OF DUST were rising on the road ahead as if cattle were stampeding. But it was a stampede of another sort. Settlers, with their household goods piled helter-skelter on wagons, were on the run and driving their livestock before them.

Soon the buckboard was engulfed in sheep and milk cows and hogs and geese. Uncle Will pulled to one side of the onrushing horde and stopped a small-eyed man on a mule.

"What's going on?"

"Indians! They're on the war path and ridin' this way! Turn back!"

Chancy and Indiana exchanged quick glances. "Mercy," she whispered.

Uncle Will was unperturbed. "We're heading for Sun Dance."

"We're *comin'* from Sun Dance," said the man on the mule. "I'm the mayor, but I just resigned. The whole town almost has got up and left."

And the ex-mayor of Sun Dance was gone.

Uncle Will stopped a man driving an oxteam. "We're

looking for Miss Russell and two youngsters. Mirandy and Jamie Dundee. Can you point them out to us?"

"The young schoolmarm? You won't find them here. The boy is too sick to move and Miss Russell and Mirandy, they won't leave."

Uncle Will cracked the whip and the buckboard was soon hurtling through the dust and confusion. Before long the prairie town was before them, standing empty and silent under the Kansas sun.

Chancy had seen bigger towns, but none he was more anxious to set foot in. He reckoned they'd snatch up Mirandy and little Jamie and Miss Russell and be gone before the Indians made a nuisance of themselves. Of course, Uncle Will might want to stay and fight, being an old Indian fighter, and that would suit Chancy too.

Uncle Will kept the whip popping in the air. Soon the buckboard pulled up along the broad dirt street. There wasn't a redskin in sight. The stores, with their tall false fronts, were locked and the windows boarded up. A man with a rifle was standing on the roof of the hotel.

"Where's Miss Russell?" Uncle Will called up.

"Those that are stayin' have gone over to the new schoolhouse." He pointed to a building that stood on a slight rise at the north end of town. Uncle Will swung the buckboard around and after another moment Chancy and Indiana jumped down.

The schoolhouse door was barricaded, but a nearby window slid open. Behind it, framed like a picture, stood a slim, green-eyed woman with a shotgun in her hands.

"What in the name of common sense do you think you're doing!" she yelled at Uncle Will. Chancy and Indi-

ana were covered with dust and she hardly looked at them.
"You get those children out of town this instant."

"Why, ma'm, we just arrived."

"Indians are on the way! Now you get!"

Chancy recognized her at once, and so did Indiana. It
was Miss Russell, still young and pretty, but in a fury. She
began giving Uncle Will such a tongue lashing that they
didn't dare interrupt.

Finally Uncle Will said, "Are you the schoolmarm?"

"Yes."

"Miss Russell?"

"Yes. Now, get!"

"Ma'm, if you'll just save your fire for the redskins and
lower your eyes again, you might notice Chancy Dundee

and his sister Indiana. They're a mite dusty, but that's them — and they're standing here busting to say howdy."

Miss Russell's face went red as paint. And her fury melted into a breathless smile. "Chancy!" she gasped. "Indiana!"

They were through the window in seconds. The room was an armed camp. Four families with grown sons were staying on to fight the Indians from the schoolhouse. Suddenly everyone seemed to be talking at once.

"Where's Mirandy?"

"Where's little Jamie?"

Jamie was rolled up in blankets behind the large new potbellied stove, and burning with fever. He was asleep. But Mirandy was missing. The blacksmith and his boys were out looking for her. She was hiding for fear Miss Russell would send her away.

Chancy and Indiana approached the stove silently and gazed down at their seven-year-old brother. His cheeks were aglow with fever and his sandy hair was damp with sweat. Chancy felt a throb in his throat. He wanted to let Jamie know that they were there, that they were together again. But Jamie seemed a thousand miles off, and they spoke in whispers. "The doctor said we don't dare move him out," Miss Russell said softly.

Chancy took a deep breath and then his eye lit on the new stove, standing like a barrel on legs. Why, if *he* were looking for a place to hide —

"Mirandy!" he said. "By dogs, Mirandy, you come out of there!"

All eyes in the room turned to the stove. There was a breathless silence. And then the iron lid began to lift and there was nine-year-old Mirandy rising like a reluctant jack-in-the box.

Her eyes were large and wet, but fierce. "I *won't* go," she said, giving her pigtails a toss. "You *can't* make me leave Jamie behind!"

"Mirandy," Chancy said in a kind of awe. "You're contrary as a mule in a mud puddle. Just like Indiana. And you look like her too."

"You everlastin' scamp," Uncle Will laughed, lifting her out of the stove. "Nobody's leaving Jamie behind. There's more'n one way to fight Indians, and I know them all. Now meet your brother Chancy and your sister Indiana, and when you get time you can say hello to your Uncle Will."

It appeared to Chancy that Mirandy's eyes would jump

out of her head. She was speechless. But then Indiana gave her the tiger kitten, and soon the three Dundees were talking away merrily — being careful not to wake little Jamie.

Finally Uncle Will said, "Chancy, give the school bell a ring and come with me. We'd better look after those Indians."

The tolling of the bell brought all the men left in town. They gathered outside the schoolhouse.

"Gents," said Uncle Will, "this is your town, but maybe you'll excuse me for butting in. There are women and young'uns in the schoolhouse and if there's a lot of shooting someone is bound to get hurt. But I calculate we can handle those Indians without firing a shot. Chancy, you get up on the roof of the hotel there and yell out if you see dust from the south or the west."

Chancy wasted no time. He'd as soon fight the Indians as not. At least, he kept assuring himself he would. Once on the roof he could see for miles around. Not a redskin was in sight. Glancing back toward Abilene, he made out the great cattle herds speckling the distant prairie.

Suddenly, below him on the street, five men leaped to their horses. They rode out of town, with Uncle Will waving them on. That struck Chancy as downright astonishing. Was Uncle Will proposing to fight the Indians single-handed?

The rattle of the horsemen quickly faded away. A silence settled over the town. Uncle Will locked the buckboard inside the livery stable and came out with an armload of rawhide ropes.

"You folks in the schoolhouse!" he yelled. "Don't show your guns or fire a shot — unless you've got no choice."

One by one he threw the rawhide coils up to Chancy on the roof. And then he sat on a hitching rail in the shade and smoked a tar-black cigar.

It was well past noon, and after almost an hour Chancy began to think the Indians would never show up. Maybe they couldn't find the town, it being so small. Still, he kept his eyes peeled. He watched a blackbird come flapping down on a distant fence as if to wait for the coming battle.

Suddenly Chancy noticed brown smoke rising to the southwest. Dust! "Indians!" he shouted. "They're coming! They're coming!"

Uncle Will tossed away the butt of his cigar. He straightened the hawk's feather in his hatband and climbed to the hotel roof with Chancy. For a long moment they watched the dust rushing toward them like a ground fire.

Soon the dust turned into Indians and Uncle Will said, "Keep down and out of sight. I don't want to have to pluck arrows out of your hide."

Chancy took a last glance at the schoolhouse. It sat white and silent under the sun. Then a foxy red movement caught the corner of his eye. He peered downward and froze. Calamity stood across the street, pecking at a tuft of grass along the raised boardwalk.

"Calamity! Get back!"

The rooster went on scratching and pecking. Chancy threw his legs over the edge of the roof and dropped to the wooden awning below. Uncle Will gave him an angry shout, but Chancy didn't pause. He'd snatch up Calamity and make it to the schoolhouse before the savages plunged into town. Within seconds he had slid down an awning post to the street — and saw Indiana rush out of the school-house window.

"Get back!" Chancy shouted.

"Calamity's got loose!"

"I know that!"

Uncle Will's voice cracked like thunder. "Clear off the street! Both of you!"

Chancy and Indiana converged on Calamity, but in the sudden excitement the rooster ducked under the slat boardwalk. Chancy sprawled on his stomach and reached an arm underneath. The rooster retreated deeper beneath the walk.

"Calamity!" Chancy bristled. "Come here! Confound you, Calamity!"

"Chick, chick!" Indiana called desperately. "Here, Calamity!"

"You get back to the schoolhouse!" Chancy declared.

"No."

"By dogs, I never saw such a contrary sister!"

"Confound you both!" Uncle Will shouted, heaving a rope down the side of the hotel. "Grab hold! Hear me! That bird can take care of himself!"

Chancy could now hear the rattle of approaching hooves. He yanked Indiana across the street with him. They reached the dangling rope and Uncle Will hauled them in like fish.

His eyes were blazing. "By the eternal! If there was time I'd give you both a walloping. Heads down!"

Chancy and Indiana crouched behind the false front. "Why in tarnation did you let Calamity out of his cage?" Chancy whispered.

"Little Jamie's head looked so hot. I thought it would feel good if Calamity fanned him. Then you and Uncle Will were shouting about the Indians coming, and I forgot about him."

In a split second painted savages came surging into town, yelling and war-whooping. The sounds alone raised the hair on Chancy's scalp. He found a chink in the boards to watch through. The Indians rode bareback, racing and yelping almost to the schoolhouse and back. Then they began milling about as if disappointed to find the town abandoned.

"That's not many Indians, to my count," Chancy whispered, trying to take some hope in it.

"They'll do," muttered Uncle Will. "Fifteen. But those

don't look like Indian ponies to me. They're saddle horses."

Indiana found a chink of her own to watch through. "Poor Calamity," she said softly.

The savages slid off their mounts and burst out laughing, and Uncle Will said, "By ginger, they don't *sound* like Indians, either."

Clancy pressed his eye tight against the chink in the false front. One of the fiercely painted men below was guffawing so hard an eagle feather flew out of his hair. "Boys," he laughed, "didn't I tell you the trick would work? Just send a man ahead yelling Injun and everybody runs! Looks like the town is ours."

"By the eternal!" Uncle Will scowled. "Those aren't Indians! They're white men!"

"Give Seven-Eyes the signal," said the horse-laughing man below, "and let's help ourselves."

"Jayhawkers," Chancy breathed, looking at Indiana. "Seven-Eyes Smith and his gang."

One of the outlaws fired a rifle in the air and soon a large man driving an empty freight wagon rode through the dust into town. The gang began looting the stores. Uncle Will held his fire. The schoolhouse held its fire. The jayhawkers broke into the general store, the bank, the harness shop and the drygoods store. Soon the wagon was piling up with blankets, kegs of butter, two new saddles, bolts of cloth, canned oysters and lanterns. All the while Seven-Eyes Smith sat on the wagon seat surveying all before him like a king, and spat tobacco juice.

"Looks mean enough to eat off the same plate with a

rattlesnake, don't he?" Uncle Will said. But he hardly seemed to be paying attention to the looting below. His eyes were fixed on the prairie beyond town.

Chancy simmered. Seven-Eyes Smith and his gang were plucking the town clean. Oh, they were infernal rascals — but Uncle Will was a grand rascal, wasn't he? What was he waiting for?

"We're not going to let them jayhawkers get clean away, are we?" Chancy said finally.

"Oh, they're aiming straight for the jailhouse. Only they don't know it yet. I just hope they don't get anxious and leave ahead of time."

"Ahead of time?"

"Why, Chancy, I suddenly decided we ought to go into

the cattle business. And I declare, here come our beeves now."

Chancy had heard the distant bellowing of cattle all along without paying any more attention to it than had the outlaws themselves. But now he looked out beyond the rooftops of town and saw longhorns converging on Sun Dance like a flow of mud. Drovers, with their hats in the air, were whipping them along.

Chancy saw Seven-Eyes Smith cock his head as the sounds grew nearer. His gang was carrying loot to the wagon from all parts of town. "Boys," he yelled out. "The wagon's full enough. Sounds like an earthquake a-headin' this way. Let's disappear."

"Hold on, Seven-Eyes — there's heaps more yet, and it's ours for the takin'. Look here what I found." And the jayhawker pulled a live chicken out of his shirt.

Indiana gave a gasp. It was Calamity.

"We'll have us some rooster soup for supper," Seven-Eyes grinned. "Boys, let's ride!"

The jawhawker tossed Calamity into the wagon. Chancy and Indiana watched in quiet horror. Uncle Will cautioned them with a gesture of his hand. The outlaws rounded up their horses, Seven-Eyes Smith cracked the whip over his team, and they started out of town. But they were too late. A herd of Texas cattle came trotting around the corner, blocking the way with a wall of tossing horns. The jawhawkers spun around and started for the west end of town. At once longhorns were rushing in on them. They turned again, but now cattle were bellowing and pouring through every crevice in town. It appeared to Chancy that every cow on the prairie was on the run and heading into Sun Dance. The outlaws quickly found themselves jammed in the middle, as tightly packed as corn on the cob.

Uncle Will drew his gun. "I figured on Indians, but those jayhawkers will do. I sent the boys to spread word at the cowcamps that there was a durned fool in Sun Dance who'd pay thirty dollars a head for longhorns until his money ran out."

Indiana kept watching from the chink in the boards. "Look what Calamity has done, Chancy!"

Calamity had taken a fluttering leap and was roosting on Seven-Eyes's left shoulder. But suddenly Chancy saw the jawhawker peering up at the false front as if he sensed people up there. Seven-Eyes raised the shotgun off his lap.

"Down!" Uncle Will ordered. "He's going to blast!"

Chancy saw a desperate opportunity. At the top of his voice he yelled, *"Fan me! Fan me, Calamity!"*

Instantly the rooster's wings threshed in Seven-Eyes's face. The outlaw almost fumbled his weapon. In the next instant Uncle Will had the drop on him.

"That'll do!" he shouted. "Easy, down there! If a gun goes off those longhorns will stampede and we'll have to scrape you boys up with a shovel. Easy. You gents ain't goin' anywhere. Now kindly toss your guns to the ground, if you can find the ground, and I'll try to get you out of that infernal mess you got yourselves into!"

The drovers were an hour making elbow room in the street. By that time Uncle Will had dropped to the wooden awning that ran over the store fronts and rescued the jay-hawkers one by one. He tossed out the rawhide lasso, pulled them up out of their saddles and hauled them in.

Indiana held the six-shooter in both hands while Uncle Will and Chancy trussed them up in bolts of calico lifted from the wagon top below. Calamity had burrowed deep under the plunder and only after the cattle were thinned out could he be rescued.

By then horse soldiers had arrived from Abilene with the news that a $1500 reward had been posted that morning for the capture of Seven-Eyes Smith and his gang. Uncle Will shoved back his hat. "Young'uns, it looks like our fortune is made," he said. "Gentlemen, you'll find the rascals stacked like cordwood on the awning, tied up pretty as you please." And then he turned back to Chancy and Indiana.

"You two are due for a hiding. But I declare, Calamity did make himself useful."

"Perishing useful," Indiana said.

"Saved our lives, most likely," Chancy added.

"Those are extenuating circumstances," Uncle Will grinned. "And Chancy, that was quick of you to get those wings flapping. By ginger, you're getting more like me every day."

"Yes, sir!"

"Now what are we going to do with all that reward money?"

The answer wasn't long in coming. The drovers were looking everywhere for the fool paying thirty dollars a head for longhorns. Uncle Will had figured the woodyard money and the clock money would buy about two beeves. But now there was the reward money. And he'd given his word.

He burst into a huge laugh. He had out-foxed himself. "Boys, that's a mighty tall price. But I never broke my word in my life," he said, and began writing out I.O.U.s. When he returned to the schoolhouse with Chancy he owned a herd of fifty Texas longhorns.

"How'll you ever sell 'em?" said Chancy.

"Why, if I can sell clocks to people who don't care what time it is, I reckon I can sell a few head of overpriced beef."

Little Jamie's fever broke that night. His eyes were open, he looked at Chancy and Indiana standing beside his bed, but they were complete strangers to him. Not even

Miss Russell could make him accept the visitors as his own kin.

For a long while Chancy found it hard to speak. Finally he smiled and dug in his pocket and held up his polished buckeye. "I brought this all the way from Ohio, Jamie. Why, if you weren't my own brother I wouldn't part with it. It's powerful good luck. It's yours, Jamie. And look here, I've got cat's eyes just like you. You can ask Indiana if that's not the truth. Cat's eyes run in our family, you know."

Little Jamie only gazed at him.

"And that's not all," said Chancy, digging in his pocket again. "See this. This is a bullet that was shot in the war. You can have it."

But Jamie didn't respond even to that and Miss Russell wiped his forehead with a damp cloth.

Finally Chancy showed off the fine four-pound axe. "See this, Jamie? This was our Pa's own axe. Imagine that! It belonged to him before you and me were born. I wouldn't be surprised if he'd want me to give it to you, being that we're brothers. Why, soon as you can jump out of bed I'll teach you how to use it. By dogs, I'll have you chopping a cord of wood in a day, same as me. Yes, sir, this axe is yours now, Jamie. Do you think I'd give you Pa's axe if you weren't my own kin?"

The gleam of the axe caught Jamie's eye. He stared at it a long while. And then his gaze slid back to Chancy and Indiana and Mirandy. A smile rose to his cat's eyes and in a dry, raspy voice he said, "How do, Indiana. Howdy, Chancy. You were a precious long time gettin' here."

"I declare," Chancy said. "If the Dundees aren't contrary they're plain contentious!"

But he was smiling. All the Dundees were together again.

"The trouble with Kansas," Jamie protested some days later, "is you can't hardly find wood to chop."

Chancy liked living on the Great Plains. But Uncle Will had changed his mind about roosting in one place. "I'm a coming-and-going man," he said that night at suppertime. "Once that herd is sold we'll be leaving, Miss Russell. You've been mighty good to care for Mirandy and Jamie, but there's a heap of places I'd like to show them."

Miss Russell turned instantly pale. "I was hoping you wouldn't take them away from me."

Chancy, Indiana, Mirandy and Jamie sat silently at the table.

"I don't want to." Uncle Will seemed unable to find a place for his eyes. "But now that they're together again I don't intend to let them get split up again."

"Why, Sun Dance is a fine place to live. It's growing every minute."

"I can see that. But it never has come natural to me to stay in one place. And you won't want a lot of young'uns around when you marry that cattleman who sent for you."

"Him!"

"Cattleman!" Mirandy blurted out. "He raised goats and smelled like 'em too."

Uncle Will cleared his throat, and Miss Russell got up for the coffeepot. Chancy hoped he would change his mind.

He liked Miss Russell. With Indiana and Mirandy and Jamie about, Sun Dance had already begun to seem like home.

The silence that had settled over the table was broken by a knock at the door. In came the blacksmith and several men of the town with broad grins on their faces.

"Excuse our walkin' in on supper," said the blacksmith, "but some news won't wait. Will Buckthorn, the folks in Sun Dance are mighty grateful to you. And you bein' a big cattleman now, why the town council — that's us — we just voted you mayor."

"Mayor!"

"The last one we had rode out of town on a mule and ain't come back. You want the job? It don't hardly pay at all, but it's mighty dignified."

Chancy had never seen Uncle Will so stunned. He couldn't find his vest pocket to put a thumb in. And then

he looked from Chancy and Indiana to Mirandy and Jamie. If he had ever hoped to see pride in their eyes he saw it now. And then his glance passed to Miss Russell. She had almost stopped breathing.

"Mayor?" he said suddenly. "Gentlemen, I've been everything from mule skinner to a clock peddler, but that's one job I never tried. Mayor, you said. Why, I calculate I'd make a fine mayor. Gentlemen, I accept. By the eternal, a family man who'd leave an up-and-coming town like this hasn't all the brains the law allows!"